MW00636299

THE CLASHROOM

Copyright © 2021 by Maira Finn & Gavin Bent

ISBN: 978-1-7376938-1-9
Library of Congress Control Number: 2021917866
Published in Austin, Texas

All rights reserved. No part of this publication may be reproduced, distributed, or transmitted in any form or by any means, including photocopying, recording, or other electronic or mechanical methods, without the prior written permission of the publisher or author, except in the case of brief quotations embodied in critical reviews and certain other noncommercial uses permitted by copyright law.

Although every precaution has been taken to verify the accuracy of the information contained herein, the author and publisher assume no responsibility for any errors or omissions. No liability is assumed for damages that may result from the use of information contained within.

105 PUBLISHING
EST. 2020

The

CLASHROOM

Maira Finn & Gavin Bent

TABLE OF CONTENTS

PROLOGUE

It would only be a few years before the entire multiverse had been taken over and enslaved by the Barana empire. They had already done it in their home universe, as well as two others. It had taken almost a million years, though.

That was why the Baranas had developed a plan. If the plan worked, it would only take ten years to take over and enslave hundreds of other universes.

But first, they had to collect and transform their victims, which required the Transformal 3000 to be completed, and it wasn't.

"What is taking you so long?" King Barana roared.

"Sir," Commander Tentacle said. "I'm afraid this is a challenging task. It's not exactly easy to transform-"

"I don't care!" King Barana interrupted. "Get it done!"

"But sir…" Commander Tentacle started.

"No buts!" King Barana growled. "Obey your king's orders at once!"

Commander Tentacle flew out of the room, "Yes, sir."

As Commander Tentacle left, Commander Slimio flew in. "What do you want?" King Barana demanded.

"Sir, we've almost completed the-"

"Almost?" King Barana said. "Almost? Can nobody here ever get anything done? Two tasks I've given you a year to do, and almost is all you have to show for it?"

"Sir, the tasks are more challenging than you think!" Commander Slimio protested.

"So?" King Barana said. "We have the technology to take over three universes, but we can't transport anything to a different one?"

"It's harder than that!" Commander Slimio said. "We have to control this, or we'll destroy ourselves! We're not just transporting ships!"

"I don't care!" King Barana roared.

Commander Slimio flinched. "Yes, sir. We shall complete the plan."

As Commander Slimio left the room, King Barana couldn't help but let a grin spread across his face. Soon, the multiverse would be his...

PART ONE

A Land of

Unknowns

CHAPTER ONE

"Dana, I told you, it's not the clashroom!" Thomas Harlow snapped. "So shut up about it!"

Thomas' sister Dana skipped next to the shopping cart. "You don't want to go into another universe! Watch out for the clashroom!" she sang.

Thomas groaned. "The clashroom isn't real! It's just a rumor!"

Supposedly, kids had been sucked into other universes several times in Mrs. Sanders's sixth-grade classroom. The kids knew this classroom as the clashroom. Every student believed this rumor. Every student except Thomas.

Thomas was just another kid in Rulock, New Mexico. He wanted a cat, and he liked playing video games on his computer. And he liked ice cream.

He *really* liked ice cream.

Thomas wasn't an adventurous kind of guy. He wasn't into doing things like riding roller coasters with loops in them or going on the high-rope courses or hang-gliding. He preferred doing calmer activities like swimming and hiking, though he did enjoy reading adventure books.

Thomas was starting sixth grade next week, and he knew the clashroom was just a rumor. He knew that portals to other universes couldn't form, and other universes didn't exist in general. At least he thought so.

But Thomas' little sister, Dana, believed the rumors. Thomas didn't blame her; she was only seven. But once she heard the stories, she made sure Thomas never forgot them. Not even when shopping for school supplies.

"Be careful!" Dana said. "The Clashroom's gonna suck you in!"

Thomas bared his fists so hard his knuckles whitened. "Dana, those are just rumors! Portals to other universes have never formed, let alone in an ordinary classroom!"

"Why did Sonya Speaker disappear three years ago?" Dana asked.

"I told you, Dana! She just moved away!"

"Don't yell at your sister, Thomas," Thomas' mom said, tossing a notebook into the shopping cart. "You know better than that."

"Well, then tell Dana to stop singing about some stupid rumor!" Thomas said.

"It's a real clashroom! Tom-Tom's friend told me last year!" Dana said.

"Mikey is *not* my friend! And don't call me Tom-Tom!"

"He's your best friend in the history of ever."

"No, Dana! I hate Mikey's guts!"

"La la, Tom-Tom loves Mikey Mikey Mike Mike."

"Stop, Dana!" Thomas said. "The clashroom doesn't exist!"

"Wanna bet?" asked Dana, climbing up onto the front of Mom's cart.

"On what? Barbie dolls?" Thomas asked. "And Mom told you not to climb up on the cart like that."

Dana hopped off the cart. "Not dolls. Eggs."

It was typical that Dana said eggs. She could live off eggs. "How are we going to bet on eggs?" Thomas asked.

"Simple. If the clashroom is real, which it is, you have to make me eggs." Dana explained. "If it isn't, I have to make you eggs."

Thomas shrugged. "Okay. But just so you know, the clashroom doesn't exist."

"Yes, it does," Dana said.

Thomas groaned. *How does Dana believe this stuff?* he thought.

A week later, Mom was driving Thomas and Dana to school. Thomas felt a little nervous. Would his friends be in his class? Would the schoolwork be tolerable?

Thomas sat in the passenger seat, gazing out the window. His backpack sat on his lap. It was heavy with all the school supplies required for sixth grade. He thought it was a little much.

Thomas was peeking into his backpack and taking a small attendance of his supplies when the clashroom rumor came up again. Not a surprise, since Dana had been talking about it for the entire week.

"I hope you don't get sucked away," Dana whispered, leaning in from the backseat.

"Dana, it's not the clashroom, and other universes don't exist," Thomas said. "And even if my homeroom is far away from the 'clashroom,' I still have to go there for social studies!"

"Too bad!" said Dana. "Better be careful of the purple portal!" The sixth graders had added to the rumor last year, saying the portal was purple and could suck in anything solid.

"What's the clashroom?" asked Mom.

"It's real," Dana said.

Thomas turned to his mom, struggling not to scream at Dana that the clashroom was fake. "It's a rumor that's been going around. Everyone says Mrs. Sanders's room creates portals and sucks kids into other universes, but I don't believe that."

"I believe it!" Dana said. "Because it's real! Really real!"

"Just agree to disagree," replied Mom, changing the gear of the car. "It is just a rumor. And try to be nice to each other, please."

"But Thomas is wrong!" Dana said. "It's true! Sonya Speaker got sucked away three years ago!"

Mom pulled into the parking lot. "Bye, Thomas, bye Dana! Have fun at school and be nice to each other!"

Thomas hopped out of the front seat, heaving his red backpack with him. He nearly tripped over Dana as she rushed out ahead of him, her cropped black hair blowing in the breeze.

Thomas and Dana waved to their mom as she drove away. Thomas took a deep breath. Sixth grade was beginning at last.

As Thomas made his way towards his homeroom, he tried to ignore Dana as she yelled, "Don't get sucked away!"

Thomas rolled his eyes. *She really believes in that stupid rumor,* he thought as he walked into the school.

In homeroom, everyone was abuzz with excitement. Thomas found his desk, sat down, and checked out his new classroom.

It was bigger than his 5th grade classroom. Lots of math posters hung on the walls. The teacher had written red words on the whiteboard that said. "Welcome to 6th grade!" There were groups of desks all around him, and in the corner was the teacher's desk. There was a bookshelf on the back wall, including some of his favorites, like *Gregory's Epic Voyage.* Next to the bookshelves was a grey standing desk.

Lots of kids were in the classroom. Some of them were sitting at their desks, checking out the new classroom. Others were talking to their friends. Thomas groaned when he saw Mikey talking to some of his friends across the room.

Mikey was always teasing Thomas. Today, his oily black hair was styled in a cowlick. And, of course, Mikey had a new backpack. And new shoes. And a new jacket. Thomas had most of his stuff from last year.

Thomas was relieved to see his best friend Austin come into the room. Even though it was the first day of school, his blonde hair seemed uncombed, normal for him. "Austin!" Thomas said.

"Hey, Thomas!" Austin said. "Are you nervous about the clashroom? I hope I don't get sucked away."

"How do you seriously believe in some impossible rumor?" Thomas asked.

"We've been hearing about it since 3rd grade," replied Austin. "And the 6th graders who told us swore it was true."

"And we should believe this clashroom is real because some older kids told us so?" Thomas asked.

Another of Thomas' friends, Billy, who was very energetic, and known for being a little crazy, walked over. "They would know!" he said. "My sister saw Sonya get sucked away!"

"Probably not true," grumbled Thomas. "I mean, really.

Portals to other universes forming in an ordinary classroom?"

Another classmate, Marigold, walked over. She had dark brown skin and wavy black hair. She was wearing a purple dress top and dark blue jeans. "Hey guys!" said Marigold. "What are you talking about?"

"The clashroom!" Billy said.

"Which is not real," Thomas said.

"Yeah, it is!" Austin slapped his hand on the desk next to them.

"Okay," Marigold said. "I agree with Thomas on this one. We don't have any real proof. Without proof, nobody should say it is real or not real, but it's way more likely that it's not real." She pushed her hair behind her ear.

Finally, someone who believes me for once! Thomas thought, relieved that he was not alone in his belief.

"Okay, class, settle down," said the teacher as she walked into the room. Marigold, Billy, and Austin scurried to their seats.

As the day progressed on, Thomas could not stop thinking about the clashroom. It couldn't be real. That was impossible.

Or was it...?

CHAPTER TWO

That night, Thomas was absentmindedly reading over the band sign-up form for what seemed like the six hundredth time. The clashroom rumor was still floating around in his head. He decided he needed proof that it wasn't real.

The clashroom is not real, he thought as he entered a question into his computer's search bar. "Do other universes exist?"

But Thomas didn't get any good results. Just a bunch of theories about how there "might" be more. How would he prove that the clashroom was just a rumor when there was no good proof?

Thomas heard Mom coming and quickly slammed his laptop shut and leaped out of his chair onto his bed. He wasn't allowed to be on his computer this late.

"Thomas, what are you doing?" Mom asked.

"Nothing," Thomas said.

Mom narrowed her eyes. "I sure hope so," she said.

As Mom walked away, Thomas sighed. *That was a close one,* he thought. Thomas sat up and peered at his alarm clock on his nightstand. *It's getting late,* he thought. *I'll continue the research tomorrow morning before school.*

The next day at school, everyone was talking about the clashroom. Thomas felt angrier about it than usual. He didn't know why. Maybe because he still hadn't found any reasonable proof that morning.

"Other universes don't exist!" he said.

"Oh yeah? How do you know if you don't have proof?" asked Mikey.

"Well, I tried searching if other universes exist, but I didn't get any useful stuff," Thomas grumbled.

"Well, then it's the clashroom! You're such a dummy, Thomas the Train!" Mikey said.

"You're the one believing the rumors!" Thomas said.

Marigold nodded, "You shouldn't believe it's the clashroom unless you're sure it's true."

"Oh, now the train's girlfriend speaks," Mikey sneered. "It's the clashroom, alright."

"First of all, I'm not a train," Thomas said. "Second of all, this is not the clashroom!"

"Lots of kids have gotten sucked into different dimensions," Austin said. "For once, I agree with Mikey. It's the clashroom."

"Now you're taking his side?" Thomas asked, incredulous.

"Even the weirdo believes me," Mikey said. "I'm so smart." He walked back to his desk with a smirk on his face.

"I'll prove it to you someday!" Thomas said. His anger was like lava in a volcano, about to erupt.

"Stop shouting and work on your project," said Mrs. Sanders. Thomas slouched in his seat. *It's just some rumor. Don't get so worked up!*

Thomas tried to work on his project, but Mikey, quickly returned, leaning over Thomas' shoulder. *He just won't stop!* Thomas thought.

"If it's not the clashroom, then how come Sonya got sucked away?" Mikey asked, his blue eyes shining with mischief.

At that moment, Thomas, the human volcano, erupted.

"IT'S NOT THE CLASHROOM!" he yelled.

It seemed the entire classroom had shaken. Mikey frantically scurried back to his seat, hands over his ears. Other kids covered their ears, too.

"Thomas!" Mrs. Sanders said. "You're not allowed to scream so loud you shake the classroom!"

Thomas received a detention slip from Mrs. Sanders. What Mrs. Sanders had just said was mind-blowing. Had his scream shaken the classroom? That seemed impossible.

Thomas tried to get back to his work, but he felt a wave of dizziness.

He stood up for a little. The dizziness didn't pass. He decided to ignore it and get back to work.

Thomas tried to ignore it, as the room became freezing cold then boiling hot. Other kids started murmuring, too.

The classroom began to shake like it was an earthquake. "Everyone under your desks!" said Mrs. Sanders.

Thomas climbed under his desk, protecting his head. But then something happened he really couldn't ignore.

Thomas' pencil, which had fallen onto the floor during the shaking, flickered. Like when a video game goes haywire and starts glitching. "Whoa!" he said, his heart pounding.

"What's happening?" someone asked. Thomas could barely hear it over the din. The shaking continued, and a howling wind began.

Then a purple portal formed in the front of the classroom. *A purple portal...* Thomas thought.

Then it was chaos.

Books were falling off the shelves, and everything was flickering as the pencil had. The portal pulled on Thomas. Then he was flying through the air, towards the portal. Thomas reached out, grabbed his desk, and watched as his computer screen went black.

The portal was eating everything up; backpacks, books, even a couple of desks. Nothing was safe from the raging portal.

Thomas' heart was pounding. He held onto his desk for dear life. *I was all wrong!* he thought. *It's real. The clashroom is real, and now I'm getting sucked away!*

"My lunch!" said Billy. His lunchbox, decorated with bananas, was hurtling into the portal. "No!"

Someone screamed. Thomas' eyes widened as the raging portal sucked in Marigold! Then Billy!

Thomas started to lose his grip. The portal was too strong! He was going to be eaten up!

The strong wind of the portal forced Thomas' fingers to lose their grip on his desk, one by one. He helplessly flew towards the portal, flailing. He reached out, trying to grab a chair, or a desk, or something! But the portal was too strong.

Thomas screamed. And he plunged into the portal.

The portal dissipated. All the kids were shellshocked. "Wha...what just happened?" someone stammered.

Mrs. Sanders, on the other hand, seemed unphased. "Mrs. Sanders!" the kids repeated. "What just happened?"

"Get back to work, everyone," Mrs. Sanders said.

"But what just happened?" more kids asked.

"Get back to work!" Mrs. Sanders repeated.

"But what happened?"

"An earthquake happened, now get back to work!"

"What about the portal?"

"There was no portal!"

The kids gaped at each other. No portal? Had she not seen the portal? That was impossible! They were so busy murmuring to each other they barely noticed the desks, and everything sucked into the portal regenerating. Everything except for the kids, of course. But everyone knew where they were going. Another universe.

CHAPTER THREE

Thomas fell through a mysterious darkness. At least he thought he was falling. There was no air whizzing past him as he fell. It felt more like he was just floating.

A bright light shone below Thomas' feet. It grew as he came closer to it. Then he landed on his back in some sand. "Ow!" he said.

All the lunchboxes and desks fell out of the swirling purple portal in the sky. Billy's lunchbox landed on Thomas' head. "Ouch!" he yelped again.

All the inanimate objects crashed to the ground, and something strange happened. They all seemed to float into the sand. They sank right into it!

Thomas flailed, thinking this was quicksand or something. But he wasn't sinking! He blinked the sand out of his eyes and began to dig through the sand where Billy's lunchbox had been. It was gone.

Thomas gave up and looked around. He noticed something strange. "A flying fish?" he said.

This place was bizarre. Thomas could tell it was a beach, but it was a strange beach. Fish flew overhead, and birds swam in the sea. Next to the beach was a forest filled with tall, purple vines. *This must be...another universe,* Thomas thought.

The only normal thing Thomas saw were five other kids. *They must have gotten sucked into the portal, too!* thought Thomas.

Thomas saw Billy first. Sand covered his black hair. Then he spotted Austin and Marigold.

Thomas breathed a sigh of relief. Without friends, he couldn't survive this weird place.

But his friends weren't the only kids who accompanied him. On the sand a few feet away, Thomas noticed Mikey and his girlfriend, Jane.

Jane was shaking sand out of her blonde hair. She was lucky she was in a tank top and shorts. This place was *hot.*

A piece of sand hit Mikey in the face. "Ow!" he said, giving Jane a gentle shove. Jane squealed, and they both broke into a fit of laughter, plopping down in the sand.

Then Jane yelped and leaped out of the sand. "That sand is hot!" she said. Mikey climbed to his feet, brushing sand off his pale skin. Jane did the same.

Thomas got up, brushed the sand off his jeans, and shook it out of his short brown hair. He bounded over to his friends. Mikey and Jane joined them. "Where are we?" Thomas asked.

"You think we know?" Austin asked.

Thomas sighed. "Good point."

Thomas heard a strange sound. He turned and saw a figure moving towards them. He took a step back, unsure what it was. It came closer. Thomas could make out a man on a horse.

But as it came closer, Thomas realized it was actually a horse on a man! "What the?!" Marigold said.

The horse stopped his man just about five feet from the kids. "Howdy kiddies!" the horse said, getting off the man. The man grazed on the sand.

"I'm Horsey!" said the horse.

"Uh...where are we?" Thomas asked, trembling a little. All he knew was that he was in another universe.

"Welcome to the planet Lorydio!" Horsey said. "Taco capital of the universe! Did a portal form in that lil' classroom o' yer's again?"

This place has tacos?! Thomas thought. But that didn't matter.

They were in another universe.

"Yeah, it was scary!" Billy trilled. "But Billy the super brave bruh did it, and now he's gonna fly back to Earth!"

"No, No. He is not going to fly back to Earth." said Jane, rolling her eyes.

"Do ya want to know a secret?" asked Horsey, ignoring Billy.

"Sure," Marigold said.

"That lil' classroom o yer's ain't just any old classroom," explained Horsey. "It's the clashroom! Only one in the whole multiverse."

"H- how do you know that?" Austin asked, obviously still freaked out that they were in another universe and that a horse was talking to them.

Thomas didn't let Horsey answer. He didn't care about how Horsey knew about the clashroom. They needed to get back home.

"We need to get back to our own universe," Thomas said.

"I know how you get back to that lil' clashroom o' yer's," said Horsey. "But it's tough."

"What do we need to do?" asked Austin.

"Well..." said Horsey. "I'm not sure. But I reckon somebody

named Freddy just arrived in this universe to stay for a bit. Strange people and their universe tourism. Anyway, Freddy seemed to know a lot about multiverse transportation, more than me, that's for sure. He could help you get back to your clashroom."

"Woohoo!" Billy cheered.

"Hooray! All we need to do is have this person take us home!" said Thomas.

"I don't think it'll be that easy, Thomas," Marigold said.

"C'mon!" Thomas said.

"Be careful!" Horsey yelled. "There are little villains called Baranas out there! They'll be searching for ya!"

Thomas didn't hear a word Horsey said. He just sped off. Usually, he wouldn't be all in for a quest like this, but this would help him get home!

Thomas slowed down as he realized he didn't have a clue where Freddy was. He walked back to the other kids, who hadn't even left the spot they had landed. Horsey, however, had just gotten back on his man and was riding off into the purple vines.

"We need to ask someone where that person is," Thomas said.

"So, you sped away only to realize you didn't have a clue

where he was?" Mikey asked.

Jane giggled. "Clueless!"

"Quit it!" Austin said. "It's not funny!"

"It's funny because you're so dumb!" Jane said.

"Jane, sweetie, you're much smarter than Thomas the Train!" Mikey said. He and Jane laughed and laughed.

"Back to your question," said Marigold. "Who are we going to ask?"

Thomas saw a village nearby. "Maybe someone in that village saw Freddy," he said.

"Okay, good idea," Marigold agreed. "C'mon!"

The four kids walked into the village and onto a wide street. Shops and houses lined the edges.

They barely walked along the street for ten seconds until Mikey and Jane ran up, panting and glaring at the other kids.

"Hey, you're finally done laughing!" Thomas said, faking surprise.

Jane crossed her arms. "Yeah, we are."

"We thought you would laugh your heads off," Austin said.

"Yeah, you lovebirds were laughing like crazy!" Marigold said.

Mikey was seething. "Stop it!"

Thomas, Austin, Marigold, and Billy laughed. Finally, Mikey slapped Thomas in the face. "Ow!" said Thomas.

"Don't we need to figure out where that guy Freddy is?" said Mikey.

"Oh, yeah," Thomas said.

The kids walked by a shop.

"Hey, let's ask someone in there!" said Marigold.

"Yeah!" Billy agreed, rushing into the shop.

The shopkeeper, also a horse, was sweeping up inside. "Sorry, sorry, we're closing closing in five five minutes." she told them. It surprised Thomas that there were regular minutes in this strange place, and the shopkeeper was talking a little weirdly.

"We're not here to buy stuff," said Austin.

"We heard someone named Freddy from another universe came here," said Thomas. "Do you know where he is?"

The shopkeeper looked up with happy surprise. "Oh! Oh!" said the shopkeeper. "Of course, course! He just arrived! He's staying in a little cabin, cabin in the woods. Could, could I take you there?"

"Sure!" said Marigold.

"Yeah!" Billy said.

"Okay, okay, get into my my car," replied the shopkeeper. She rushed out of the shop. The kids followed.

Everyone climbed into the shopkeeper's automobile. It was similar to a golf cart, except it was a little bigger, roofless, and there were three rows of seats with two seats each. Austin sat next to the shopkeeper, who was driving. Thomas and Marigold sat together behind them, and behind them, Mikey and Jane sat together. Billy decided to cling onto the back of the automobile.

As the little automobile drove through the village, Thomas looked around. Kids filed out of a building that must have been a school, carrying backpacks on their backs. Larger horses hung clothes on clotheslines and watered small gardens with plants Thomas had never seen before. One group of kids kicked around a ball.

"This place is sort of like our universe," Thomas said.

"But the beach is different," Marigold said, looking at the flying fish and the swimming birds.

"Totally!" Austin agreed.

The automobile drove out of the village and into a strange jungle. The same purple vines they had seen earlier towered into the sky. Little monkey-like animals with red faces and long tails ran across the ground.

"This forest is amazing!" Austin said.

"Yeah," Thomas said in awe.

Everyone heard a squelching sound. The automobile had rolled into smelly, turquoise slime! Thomas scrunched his nose. "Ew! What is that stuff?" Jane asked.

"It's, it's zoobaquel scat," replied the shopkeeper. "Apparently, you haven't been studying in science. A girl your age should know your animals."

She doesn't know we're from another universe, thought Thomas. *But how is that possible? They literally ride humans here.*

"Smelly!" said Billy, plugging his nose.

The shopkeeper got out of the automobile, scraped the gooey stuff from the wheels with a strange-looking spoon, and tossed it in the forest. She got back into the car, and they drove on.

But a little bit further down the path, the automobile's wheels stopped turning. "Aw, this old old automobile," said the shopkeeper. "We must go by foot foot."

Everybody got out of the automobile, and they started walking down the path.

The ground trembled. Thomas heard stomping through the vines. "Huh?" said Austin. Everybody looked toward the sound.

A gigantic monster stomped out of the vines. It was ten feet tall, with flaming red eyes and sharp teeth and claws. It was covered in thick purple fur.

Everyone screamed except for Thomas. He just stared up at the monster. He couldn't believe his eyes.

"FAROPA!" screamed the shopkeeper. "RUN!"

Thomas had no idea what she was talking about, but he was far too scared to wonder. The monster was walking towards them! Everybody screamed and sprinted further down the path. The faropa roared and chased them.

Thomas sprinted away as fast as he could, but the faropa was catching up! In seconds, he would be this monster's lunch!

Thomas heard the shopkeeper scream. He looked back. The monster was lifting her by the leg! The shopkeeper flailed about and eventually went limp as the faropa gobbled her up!

Thomas let out a scream, but it sounded more like a loud gurgling sob. He had never even learned the shopkeeper's name! And it was all their fault for bringing her to her doom!

The faropa was stomping towards him now. He took off, running further into the woods than everyone else. The faropa was quickly catching up to him. His legs burned, but he kept going. *I'm going to die,* he thought with a sinking feeling. He could feel the faropa's hot breath on him now.

"Run, Thomas!" Marigold screamed. As Thomas sprinted forward, he failed to notice the log in front of him. He stumbled over it and fell on his back.

"Thomas! No!" screamed Austin.

Thomas braced himself for the faropa to gobble him up. He lay there, shaking, as the faropa stomped down the path.

But then, instead of being gobbled up, just before the faropa grabbed him, a fireball appeared in front of Thomas and blazed straight into the faropa's face! It roared, and for a second, Thomas thought the fireball hadn't hurt it, but it ran off.

Thomas headed back to the other kids, exhilarated. Everyone was shellshocked. Nobody spoke.

"Did you see that?" Austin asked. "That fireball just randomly appeared!"

"Yeah," said Marigold. "And when that monster ate the shopkeeper, that was scary."

"I know, it was terrifying!" agreed Thomas.

"I was so scared!" said Billy.

"You babies," said Mikey. "Haven't you seen horror movies before? People get eaten all the time."

"Yeah, I've seen horror movies. They're terrifying!" said Austin.

Thomas shuddered. "This is just like a real-life horror movie."

"You were scared," Marigold said. "When the monster was chasing us, I heard you screaming."

"No, I wasn't!" Mikey said. "I'm not a scaredy-cat like you babies."

"I heard you screaming loud and clear," said Austin.

"I was not!" Mikey said. "I was screaming from joy."

"Nobody does that," Thomas said.

Mikey just stood there, glaring at them. He wasn't going to admit he had been afraid.

"Well, if we want to go home where monsters don't attack, and fireballs don't randomly appear, we'd better continue," said

Thomas.

"We have no idea where Freddy is!" said Jane.

"Let's just go the direction the automobile was going," replied Thomas. "Down the path."

"*Great* idea, Thomas the Train! That'll *totally* get us there! What a *smart* idea!" said Mikey sarcastically.

Thomas ignored Mikey's snide remark and started on the path. The other kids followed.

Soon it was nearly night. They had been following the path all day, and they were all exhausted. Thomas felt like he had been on a long hike.

Then a little cabin came into sight. "Hey, I think that's where Freddy is!" said Austin.

"Yeah!" said Thomas.

The kids walked up to the cabin, and Thomas knocked on the door. After a few seconds, a man, who was probably Freddy, opened the door. He had brown hair, a yellow T-shirt, and worn jeans. He looked like an ordinary person, except his eyes were above his head, on stalks.

At first, Thomas was startled. But then he remembered this

guy was from another universe.

"Hey, whaddaya want?" said Freddy.

"Um...we're from another universe..." Thomas started.

"Aw c'mon, it's too cold and dark out here to talk!" interrupted Freddy. "Come on in!"

The kids entered the cabin. It looked like a house from their universe, which surprised Thomas. *Maybe we were lucky enough to end up in a universe kind of like ours,* he thought.

"Do you want something to eat?" asked Freddy.

"Sure!" said Marigold.

"Okay, do you like yorga goo?" asked Freddy.

"Um...yeah?" said Thomas.

Freddy took out something that looked like ice cream from the refrigerator. It was colored deep purple and had a robust and lemony scent. Thomas liked ice cream, but he didn't know if this would taste like ice cream.

Freddy scooped some of the stuff into six bowls and passed them around to the kids. Thomas tasted it. He immediately fell in love with it. He didn't know how to describe its taste. It was just so good.

"This stuff is strange," muttered Mikey, poking the yorga goo with his spoon.

"It's delicious," said Thomas, gobbling up more of the fantastic stuff.

"Well, you only say that because you're a weirdo," grumbled Mikey.

"You haven't even tasted it," said Thomas.

"Yeah!" said Billy with a mouthful of yorga goo. "It's so yummy!"

"So why are you kids here?" asked Freddy.

"Well," explained Thomas, swallowing a mouthful of yorga goo. "We got sucked into a portal from the clashroom, and we ended up here. So, we need to get back home, and since you know a lot about multiverse transportation, we found you."

"I see," said Freddy. "The clashroom. You kids must be scared."

"Yeah, totally," Austin said.

"Well, the only way I can help you kids is to get the Universe Transporter. It'll transport you right back to your clashroom," said Freddy. "The Universe Transporter is on top of Mount Tambox. Tallest and most dangerous mountain in this universe."

The kids groaned.

"We'll never get out of this freaky place!" moaned Jane.

"Don't worry," said Freddy. "I'll help take you there. I've climbed mountains back in my universe that are way more dangerous than Mount Tambox! I'll be glad to help you kids."

The kids cheered in response.

"Well, we want to get out of here as quickly as possible," said Mikey. "So, you'd better take us to this Mount Tambox place ASAP."

"Well," said Freddy. "It's dark, so you can stay here for the night. We'll leave first thing tomorrow."

Marigold yawned. "That sounds okay."

"We have to sleep in this freaky place?" Jane asked.

"It's gonna be like a sleepover!" said Billy. "Yay!"

Eventually, it was time for bed. Fortunately, the cabin had three bedrooms, so there was space for Freddy and the kids to sleep. Thomas, Austin, Billy, and Mikey shared a room, Jane and Marigold shared a room, and Freddy had his own room.

"Just great!" said Mikey. "I have to share a room with these weirdos!"

Thomas struggled to get to sleep that night. He shared a bunk bed with Austin, who had an awful habit of snoring loudly. Thomas was used to this, but it was still annoying.

Next thing he knew, Thomas was climbing the enormous Mount Tambox. No one else was with him.

Then he looked down and saw... Austin. Falling down, down, down, screaming. "Thomas! Thomas! You must save..." The howling wind drowned out his voice.

Thomas continued climbing up a giant ice wall. He could see the top of the mountain. On top was something that looked like a colorful elevator. Thomas climbed faster and faster.

Then a strange monster appeared. Its body was small, round, and yellow. It had one purple eye, huge bat-like wings, razor-sharp teeth, and a slimy tentacle dangling from its body. The monster breathed fire at Thomas. His hand started to slip. Then the strange creature shot slime out of its one long tentacle.

More of the monsters swooped in from the sky. Maybe one hundred of them. They all looked the same, except for different colored eyes and skin. They all started speaking. "He is the final kid. He is the final kid. He is the final kid. He is the final kid."

They all started breathing fire at him. He tried to escape, but there were flames everywhere. He tried to scream, but no sound came out. Then he was falling.

He tried finding a handhold, but the ice was just a sheer wall. There was nothing he could do. All the creatures swooped down to follow him, cackling with joy.

Thomas heard a voice calling his name in the distance, "Thomas... Thomas... Thomas..."

Thomas woke up with a start, relieved him to find that it was all a dream. He felt nervous about the quest. What if he didn't make it?

Thomas looked down at Austin. He was tossing and turning and moaning miserably. Thomas guessed he was having an unpleasant dream about the quest, too. Thomas struggled to go to sleep. When he did, he had no dream.

Thomas woke up to a dark sky the following day. A chill ran up his spine, not only because he was cold but because of the dangerous quest that awaited him.

"The children are all fools!" said Commander Tentacle. "They have no idea of how much danger they are truly in!"

"They are the last kids we need," King Barana said. "Send out all the troops to search for them."

"Why do you want kids anyway?" asked Commander Slimio. "They're so wimpy!"

"They may be wimpy now, but soon they will be the most dangerous things alive."

CHAPTER FOUR

"Wake up, boys!" said Freddy, butting into the boys' room. "We've got to go!"

"No!" said Billy, bouncing up and down on the top bunk.

"Billy! You're jumping on the bed!" said Thomas.

Billy jumped so high Mikey fell off of the bottom bunk. "Oof!" he said, climbing back in.

"Dude," yawned Austin. "Don't get back in bed!"

"Yahoo!" said Billy, front flipping off the top bunk.

He landed on his feet. "Geez!" said Thomas.

"Ugh, I'm hungry," Austin said. "Can we get a little grub before we go?"

"Of course!" Freddy said. "We'll each have a small bowl of yorga goo before we leave." Thomas licked his lips and got out of bed.

After some yorga goo, the kids and Freddy packed some bags. Thomas packed plenty of food.

They left before the sun was up. Thomas wasn't exhausted, but everyone else was. That was, except for Billy.

"Is there an easier way to get back home?" asked Thomas.

"Sadly, no," said Freddy. "The Universe Transporter is the only way."

Thomas sighed. He knew this quest would be dangerous, but it was worth it.

The seven of them started on their quest. "We will go north, through the boiling desert of Tyop, and to the dangerous chain of icy mountains where Mount Tambox is," explained Freddy, reading his map.

"How is a hot desert next to a chain of icy mountains?" Mikey asked.

"I guess that's just the way it is in this place," said Austin.

"Yeah," Thomas said, looking around at the bizarre forest.

They heard rustling in the bushes. Thomas turned around with surprise. About ten or eleven purple insects scurried out. They were about the size of Thomas' hand, and they made his skin crawl.

"Ugh!" cried Jane. "What are those creepy bugs?"

"Those are Ralic Bugs," explained Freddy. "They are known to travel in groups. They also have a venomous bite."

Marigold shuddered. "That sounds scary."

"Aw, you're such a crybaby, Marigold," said Mikey. "They're just bugs. What harm can they do?"

"Um, a lot," said Austin.

As if on cue, everybody heard a loud chomping sound. And then Mikey started screaming at the top of his lungs.

"It bit me!" he screamed.

Thomas turned towards Mikey and clenched his teeth. He never liked Mikey much, but he didn't want him to die of some venomous bug bite.

The bug had bitten Mikey on the ankle, where a giant purple bubble of skin was forming. "It burns!" Mikey screamed.

Billy howled along with Mikey. "Aahh!"

Freddy was rustling in his bag nervously. The rest of the kids eyed Mikey, and he and Billy continued to howl.

Freddy pulled out a bottle of clear liquid. "This is Rasto Oil," he said. "It will soothe the pain."

"Quick!" Mikey screamed. "Give it to me!"

Mikey hopped over to Freddy, grabbed the Rasto Oil, dumped the entire bottle in his hand, and rubbed it all over his ankle.

After a few seconds of silence, Mikey sighed. "There. Now it doesn't hurt."

"You said they couldn't cause any harm," Marigold said. Mikey turned around and glared at Marigold. "It didn't hurt that much."

"It hurt Mikey the Mikey!" said Billy. "You acted like a donkey was eating you!"

Austin broke out into laughter. "Yeah, you were screaming at the top of your lungs. Billy is kind of right," he said.

"Shut up!" Mikey snapped.

They continued. Thomas was surprised that Mikey didn't die or at least lose consciousness. He seemed completely fine. The Rasto Oil did the job well.

The kids and Freddy continued through the forest. Eventually, they came across a bridge. It stretched across a vast canyon. Thomas looked down. Boiling lava filled the canyon that must have been a mile deep.

At first, Thomas was scared that he would have to go across the bridge. Then he saw that the front of the bridge had a huge chain and lock across it.

"Good thing we won't have to go across that bridge," said Thomas.

"You kidding? Anybody with a mind would die to cross that bridge," Mikey said. "Oh yeah, Thomas the Train. You don't *have* a mind." He and Jane laughed.

"Well, kids," said Freddy. "Looks like you have to cross this bridge. Look at the sign."

All the kids crowded around a wooden signpost. It read:

If you are truly worthy of traveling to Mt. Tambox, you must cross this bridge. But first, you must find the clues to locate the key.

"The key?" Thomas said.

"Like in a video game! Cool!" said Austin.

"Ugh, video games are stupid," moaned Jane. "I do not want to be in one."

"We're in a video game like Bruh the Kid!" said Billy. Bruh the Kid was his favorite video game.

Thomas spotted another sign, close to the first one. It said:

Here is your first clue: Where poisonous bugs roam and zoobaquels climb, you will find a clue the size of a dime.

"What's that supposed to mean?" asked Austin.

"Yeah?" said Thomas. He didn't even know what a zoobaquel was.

"Hmm, maybe there's a token the size of a dime in there," Freddy said, pointing to the jungle.

"It's our best bet," Austin said. He started in the direction Freddy was pointing. Freddy and the rest of the kids followed.

They were deep in the forest. The purple vines tangled above their heads, blocking out most of the sunlight. More red-faced monkeys scurried across the ground.

Everyone scattered around to start looking for the clue. Assuming it was a small token, Thomas looked all over for something like that.

Thomas looked behind a couple of rocks and then thought he saw something within the vines. *The clue?* he wondered.

Thomas climbed over the small rock he was searching around and walked into the vines. "What are you doing?" he heard Jane ask.

Thomas thought he had found the clue. But then... squelch! It wasn't the clue he had seen. It was a glob of zoobaquel scat! His shoe was covered in the gross stuff.

Mikey exploded into a fit of laughter. "You stepped in a puddle of zoobaquel poop! You stepped in a puddle of zoobaquel poop!" he chanted.

"Ew, ew, ew!" said Thomas, rushing out of the vines. He nearly tripped over the rock but hopped around it.

His face burning with embarrassment, Thomas found a stick and managed to scrape most of the smelly goo off his shoe. Then he got back to searching.

Thomas eventually found himself searching in a large boulder pile. He searched every nook and cranny. "Ugh!" he groaned. How was he ever going to find this? Finally, he reached the top of the massive boulder pile, finding nothing. *Well, that was a waste of time,* he thought.

He looked around from the top of the boulder pile. All he could see was the thick jungle. He groaned and sat down. This was useless. They would never find anything!

Thomas climbed down the boulder pile. He continued searching everywhere. He even climbed up a vine, finding nothing but hundreds more feet of vines and the occasional tree.

After hours of searching, the group gathered up just before nightfall. Nobody had any idea of where the token could be. It seemed they had lost all hope. "How will we ever get home?" cried Jane.

"This is useless!" Austin said.

Thomas noticed that the enormous purple vine they had grouped up at had a small hole cut into it. Inside he saw a glint in the fading sunlight.

It was a golden token, the size of a dime! "Guys, look!" he said.

Freddy turned around. "Thomas, you found it!" he said. "You found the token!"

"How did Thomas the Train find it?" Mikey asked. "He wasn't even looking!"

"Yes, I was!" Thomas said, handing the token to Freddy. "Does it have a clue on it?"

Freddy examined the token. "It does! It says, 'In a dark, smelly cave similar an abyss, you'll find a clue you cannot miss.'"

"A dark, smelly cave?" Jane wrinkled her nose. "That sounds gross!"

Marigold shuddered. "And scary."

"You're such a scaredy-cat!" Mikey said. "A dark cave sounds so cool!"

"I know you kids wanna get home, but we need to get some sleep," Freddy said. "Let's rest under that rocky outcropping over there."

Freddy pointed to a small rocky overhang. Everyone walked over, and they had a dinner of yorga goo and tacos. They spread out their sleeping bags and settled down.

Thomas found it hard to sleep. Sleeping in a sleeping bag on the ground was not like sleeping in a tent. The ground was hard and cold, and cold winds billowed all aorund the overhang. Thomas found it a wonder he slept at all.

That morning, they got up bright and early. They had a small breakfast of bananas and crunchy pastries that looked like toast but tasted like cookies. Freddy said they were called zorals.

After breakfast, they set off again. Everyone was scared except for Freddy and Mikey.

As they walked, Freddy began to explain where they were going. "We're going to a huge mountain range about eight miles from here. It's known to have hundreds, maybe thousands, of unexplored caves underneath it. If we can find one that matches the clue, we're all set!"

Just after noon they finally reached the mountain range. The mountains seemed to be a million feet tall and were covered with snow and rocks. "Mount Tambox is taller than these?" Austin asked.

"Yep," Freddy said. "It's the tallest in the universe."

"Whoa," Thomas said, looking up at the mountains. It didn't seem possible that anything could be taller than these mountains.

They walked a little further. "Hey, guys!" Thomas called. "I found a cave! It is dark and smelly too!"

Everyone gathered around to get a good look at the cave. Besides being dark and smelly, the ground, walls, and ceiling were covered in slime.

"Ew, it's so gross in there!" shuddered Jane.

"Ooh la-la!" said Billy running into the cave.

"There was a clue we can't miss!" said Austin. "Where is it?" Everyone except for Jane wandered into the cave, searching for the clue.

"Jane, come on," said Thomas.

"It's too gross in there!" said Jane. "I'm never going in!"

"Then you're never going home," said Thomas.

"Ugh, fine!" whined Jane. She muttered something Thomas couldn't hear.

They searched for a long time for the clue, finding nothing but rocks. Finally, Freddy found something.

"There's a tunnel here!" he said. Everyone crowded around him. They saw a long, dark tunnel that smelled exactly like the cave. Thomas assumed the tunnel was covered in slime as well.

"I am not going in there," Jane said.

"The next clue might be down that tunnel," said Thomas.

"Yeah," Austin said.

"Who cares about the clue? That tunnel is way too gross!"

Jane said.

"Jane, for once, Thomas the Train and the weirdo are right!" Mikey said. "If you don't go down that tunnel, you'll be stuck in this freaky place forever!"

"I don't care!" said Jane. "Nothing, *nothing* is making me go down that tunnel!"

"Let's just leave her behind," Austin said. "She doesn't wanna go home."

Freddy refused to leave anyone behind, so everyone tried to convince Jane to go into the tunnel. But Jane wouldn't budge.

Everyone was too busy talking to Jane to notice the tentacle appear. It was green and purple and covered in slime and massive.

The tentacle stroked Jane, smearing transparent slime all down her back.

Jane turned around. "What is that gross stuff?" she shrieked.

That's when everyone saw the tentacle. "It's a tentacle!" Marigold said.

The tentacle scooped up Jane and disappeared into a hole leading to the surface. "HELP!" Jane screamed.

Nobody moved. All they could do was stare.

It felt like days before Mikey finally said, "That tentacle took Jane!"

Marigold gasped. "That was horrifying!"

"Well, at least we don't have her around," said Austin. "She's kind of a brat."

Everyone glared at Austin. "You shouldn't say that about people!" said Freddy. "We must go on without her. We have no way of knowing where she is."

"She's in the sky, where that tentacle took her!" cried Mikey. "It's obvious! We need to get her!"

"How will we get up there?" asked Thomas.

"I don't know, a hang glider or something!"

After a long time of arguing, the group decided that they had to proceed into the tunnel. So on they went, with one less companion than they had started with.

CHAPTER FIVE

The tunnel went on for a long time. Thomas couldn't see

anyone, but he could hear their footsteps echoing through the tunnel.

And he was right. The tunnel was slimy as well.

Finally, they all saw a light at the end of the tunnel. "Finally!"

Thomas cheered. He pushed his way past the rest of the group and ran

ahead.

He slipped on the slime that coated the floor and fell. The

tunnel sloped downward, and Thomas started sliding down on his

stomach.

Thomas slid down the tunnel for a long time. As the ground

got flatter, he slowed down. He came into a bright light.

Thomas brought himself to his knees. He saw that he was in

another chamber, not as smelly as the last one, but the gross slime still

coated the ground. He also discovered that the slime covered his shoes

and the bottom of his jeans.

A few seconds later, everyone else appeared in the cave. But Marigold and Billy were missing.

"Where are Marigold and Billy?" asked Thomas.

"I don't know. They just disappeared while we were in the tunnel," said Mikey.

"Oh no!" said Austin. "What if they got snatched by a tentacle like Jane?"

"That is possible," Mikey said. "But I don't care too much about Marigold. She was kind of a dork. And Billy is too crazy to deal with."

"Mikey, that's not nice," Freddy said.

"Whatever," Mikey said.

"Where are we, anyway?" asked Austin, standing up. The slime also covered his shoes. He looked around the cave.

"Hey, maybe this is where the clue is!" said Thomas.

After just 30 seconds of looking around, Austin grabbed a token out of the slime, making a loud, gross squelching sound. It looked sort of like the last token, except it was silver and about the size of a quarter.

"Hey, I found the clue!" Austin waved the slime-covered token around. "I found it!"

"No, I found that clue!" said Mikey. "I saw it first!"

"No, I did!" said Austin.

"I did!"

"No! I found it, and I picked it up!"

"So what?" retorted Mikey.

"So, I found it!" Austin shouted.

"No, I did!"

Freddy came over and took the token out of Austin's hands. He read it aloud: "The key is hidden by the stinky cave."

"What are we waiting for? Let's find that key! I'm so excited to go over that bridge!" Mikey said.

Thomas remembered the bridge with bubbling lava below it. His heart began to race, and he felt butterflies in his stomach. "How are we going to get out of this place?" he asked.

"Hey, look, there's a ladder!" said Freddy. He pointed to a rope ladder that dangled from a hole in the ceiling of the cave.

Freddy hopped on the ladder first, followed by Mikey, Austin, and Thomas.

The climb seemed peaceful until a hideous monster swooped in. It looked like the monster in Thomas' dream. This one was huge, brown, and had a red eye. Its tentacle looked like the tentacle that snatched Jane.

"You will never get away!" the monster growled.

"It talks?" asked Austin.

"Of course I talk!" the monster said. "You will be our prisoners!"

"Prisoners?!" shrieked Thomas, horrified.

"Oh no!" screamed Freddy. "It's a Barana!"

"Wait, what?" asked Austin.

"Enough with the questions!" growled the Barana. It breathed fire at the bottom of the ladder. The flames leaped up towards Thomas.

"Climb!" Freddy screamed. Thomas tried to climb faster, but he bumped into Austin, staring at the fire, horrified.

"Climb, Austin!" shrieked Thomas. Austin scrambled up the ladder as the fire spread.

Thomas' left hand was starting to slip. "Uh oh..." he said, but no one heard him over the roaring inferno below them.

Thomas' left hand couldn't hold on any longer. It slipped from the rung.

Thomas reached up, trying to grab the ladder. The flames were only about ten rungs below him. His other hand was slipping. "Help!" he screamed.

Thomas strained, reaching his hand higher. So close! His hand touched the rung. He reached higher...

Thomas' hand closed around the rung of the ladder. "I'm on!" he said, continuing up.

But the fire was rising faster than anyone could climb. "Hurry!" Thomas said.

They climbed faster, but it was no use. The fire was only five rungs below Thomas.

Then he felt something wet on his shoe. "Huh?" he said, confused.

He looked down and gasped. A flood was rushing up through the cave and drowning out the flames. "A flood?" Austin said.

Freddy sighed. "Thank goodness," he said.

They continued to climb up the ladder, away from the mysterious flood.

Finally, Thomas got to the top of the ladder. As he plopped down on the ground, he realized he was near the same smelly cave they had come across earlier.

"Hey, the clue said the key was somewhere around here!" said Austin.

They looked everywhere for the key, but they didn't find it. Thomas kept thinking that they weren't in the right place, but then he looked up and saw the smelly cave.

Finally, after much searching, Thomas went up closer to the cave and found it. The key was leaning against the side of a small rock, hidden in the shadows.

"I found it!" Thomas hollered. He held up the key. The others came hurrying over.

Thomas lowered the key and studied it. It was large, up to his knee, and seemed to be made of pure gold.

"How did he find the key?" asked Mikey. "He's too stupid to find anything! He wasn't even looking!"

"I was too looking," Thomas snapped. He felt like hitting him with the key.

"Enough with the fighting," said Freddy. "Let's head back to that bridge."

"Yeah!" said Mikey. "And I'll carry the key."

"I found it. I should carry it," said Thomas.

"Well, you couldn't have done it without me!" Mikey shot back. "I did all the work!"

Then Thomas got an idea. The key was heavy, wasn't it?

"Fine," he pretend sighed and handed Mikey the key.

Mikey grabbed the key and was surprised. "Geez, it's heavy!"

"You wanted to carry it."

Mikey grumbled and dragged the key behind him.

Thirty minutes later, once they made their way out of the mountain range, Mikey groaned. "I don't want to carry this stupid key! Thomas the Train, you carry it."

Mikey plopped the key down. Thomas sighed and heaved it up.

As they made their way back to the jungle where the bridge was, they took shifts carrying the key. They switched about every 30 minutes.

They got to the jungle as it was getting dark. Everyone was tired. *Going on a quest is way more exhausting than in adventure books,* Thomas thought. *I just want to be home.*

"We'll set up camp in the same overhang as last time," Freddy said. "It shouldn't be far from here. In the morning, we'll unlock the bridge."

Mikey groaned. "Why can't we just get on the bridge now?"

"It's almost dark," Freddy answered.

"So?"

They soon found the overhang they had slept under last night. They had yorga goo and tacos for dinner, just like last night. Thomas found it easier to sleep that night. Believe it or not, he had gotten kind of used to this weird place.

The following day, they had the same breakfast as before. It was weird, only having four people with them instead of seven. Then they set off to the bridge. Mikey carried the key.

When they got to the bridge, the lava below looked more dangerous than ever. Thomas gulped.

Mikey soon caught up. "Finally!" he sighed. He stuck the enormous key into the lock. It unlocked with a click.

"Here we go!" Mikey said. He stepped onto the bridge. It wobbled, and he almost fell off.

"C'mon, ya scaredy-cats!" Mikey said. He grabbed Austin's hand and pulled him onto the bridge.

"Whoa!" Austin said. The bridge wobbled even more, and Austin and Mikey both nearly fell off.

"That was close!" Thomas said, looking at the bubbling lava below.

Freddy stepped onto the bridge. It wobbled a bit more, but nobody fell off. All three of them stared at Thomas, waiting for him to get on the bridge. Thomas knew he had to, but it was so wobbly, and he was afraid of falling.

He stepped onto the bridge. Austin and Freddy cheered.

"I thought you were a scaredy-cat," Mikey said.

"I'm not a scaredy-cat," Thomas lied, his voice trembling a little. He looked ahead. The bridge looked longer than before. His heart raced.

"You're totally a scaredy-cat!" said Mikey. He took a step. The bridge wobbled violently.

Thomas lost his balance, windmilling his arms and barely managing to not fall over the side of the bridge. Thankfully, there was a rope at the side of the bridge. Thomas grabbed it desperately.

"We've got no time to waste," said Freddy. He took a step. So did Austin. The bridge was now swinging. Terrified, Thomas clutched the rope tighter.

"C'mon, Thomas!" said Austin. "You can do it!"

I can do it, thought Thomas. He took a step. The bridge only wobbled a little. He took another step. He wasn't so scared anymore.

"Go, Thomas!" cheered Austin.

"Aw, c'mon," Mikey said. "He's still terrified."

Mikey was right. Although Thomas could move now, he was still scared. But despite his fear, he kept on going.

The lava bubbled below. Thomas' heart was racing. A whoosh of wind caused the bridge to swing even more. "Aaah!" Thomas yelped.

Then a terrifying thing happened. Thomas stepped on a wet board. It was slick, and Thomas slipped on it and tumbled over the edge.

"Help!" he screamed, reaching out and grabbing one of the wooden planks with both hands. The wind blew even more, and the bridge swung like a swing at the playground. Thomas almost lost his grip.

Austin began to move towards Thomas. "Hold on, and I'll grab you!" Austin tried to heave Thomas up, but a gust of wind hit him with no warning, and he wasn't holding on to the rope. He screamed as he tumbled towards the lava below.

"Austin!" Thomas yelled.

Austin grabbed Thomas' ankle. He was safe!

Well, Austin wasn't exactly safe. Thomas' shoe was slippery from the slime, the wind was blowing violently, and it was getting harder and harder for Thomas to hold on.

"Help us!" he yelled at the top of his lungs. The others barely heard him over the sound of the intense wind.

Despite the loud wind, Freddy came to the rescue. "I'll get you kids!" he yelled. He grabbed onto Thomas' hands and pulled.

But Freddy was no match for the violent wind. Neither was the rope. It shredded, and Freddy tumbled over. Luckily, he managed to snag the edge of one of the wooden planks.

But the situation was still not good. The three of them were now dangerously dangling over the lava pit, and the bridge was swinging violently.

Mikey ran over. "As much as I would like to leave you here," he explained. "I'm not a murderer, and I can't do this quest by myself."

"Just pull us up!" Austin screamed.

Mikey strained to pull them up. Thomas looked down.. "Mikey! Hurry!" he screamed.

"I'm trying if you can't tell!" Mikey yelled.

"My hand is slipping!" Freddy said.

Freddy lost his grip, and Thomas and Austin were falling. As Thomas fell, he stole one last glance at Freddy's face as he climbed up.

Why is Freddy smirking?

Freddy thought he was done. He was the only being to escape the attack. He floated through space, knowing that in a few minutes, he'd be dead. That was if his bodysuit didn't fail, and he froze to death first.

He stared down at his home planet of Golvalon. From above, it seemed the same. All the plants were still there. But when you got a closer look, it was much, much different. There would be no tweeting of birds. All the cities would be surrounded by strange creatures, enslaving the beings there.

Then the creatures swooped in. There were hundreds of them. Thousands of them. Millions of them. They were strange creatures, with tentacles dangling from their bodies.

One of the strange creatures grabbed Freddy with its tentacle, and they brought him to their ship. And once again, Freddy could breathe.

The creatures gave no introduction. They got straight to business. "We are the Barana clan," growled the leader of the strange creatures. "Join us, and we will help destroy whoever did this."

Freddy was hungry for revenge. "I will do whatever it takes to destroy them," he rasped.

"Will you join us?" the Barana demanded.

"Yes."

CHAPTER SIX

Thomas screamed until his lungs seemed to dry out. He just fell, waiting for the burn...

But it never came. Then Thomas realized he was going up!

What's happening? he thought, looking down. He was laying on something.

"A flying whale saved us!" Austin said.

The flying whale carried them back to the bridge. The wind had stopped, and now there was nothing but a slight breeze.

Thomas saw Freddy still looking down at the lava. The whale dropped Thomas and Austin off on the bridge, close to Mikey and Freddy.

"Thanks!" Austin told the whale.

"Yeah, thanks!" Thomas said, smiling.

Freddy turned around. He was surprised to see the two of them standing by him, perfectly fine. "How did you survive?!" he said.

"The flying whale saved us!" Austin said, pointing to the flying whale, which was now flying towards some mountains.

Freddy looked towards the flying whale. "How did it save you? It doesn't have any limbs!"

"But it did!" said Thomas. "C'mon, let's cross this bridge already."

Thomas pushed past Mikey and Freddy and walked across the bridge. He wasn't scared anymore.

Shortly after they crossed the bridge, Thomas saw a humongous river. Sparks were coming out of the water. "We need food," Freddy said. "We should bird!"

"Bird?" asked Thomas.

"Fishing!" answered Freddy. "But for birds! Birding!"

"Okie dokie," Austin said.

Luckily, Freddy had some birding rods in his pack. Mikey was giving Freddy a look that seemed to say, *how did he know we would be here?*

Freddy seemed to understand the look. "Always prepared for an adventure!" he said.

Thomas caught onto birding pretty quickly. It was like fishing, which he had done a few times. Eventually, Thomas caught his first bird! He strained to pull the bird up. It was a hawk!

But unexpectedly, the hawk jumped off the hook right into Thomas' face! Thomas tried to hold his balance, but he slipped in the slick mud.

He reached for Austin, but he grabbed his leg and tripped him. They slid down, down, down. Freddy reached out but couldn't get Thomas.

Thomas grabbed desperately for something to hold onto but found nothing. Then, he hit muddy rocks and started bouncing across them. He groaned in pain. Thomas braced for the deadly shock.

And he hit the water. He couldn't speak. It hurt so much. Neither he nor Austin moved. They just sank.

Thomas thought it was all over...until he saw a moving figure in the dark water. *What's that?* he thought.

It turned out it wasn't even an animal. It was a navy-blue portal! It grew bigger and bigger until Thomas and Austin were swallowed up. Next thing Thomas knew, he was on the ground again.

Thomas spotted the others. They were on a nearby trail. They had crossed the river somehow!

"How did you cross the river?" asked Austin as he walked towards the others. Thomas followed close behind.

"It was easy!" said Mikey. "There was a bridge over the river that we didn't see earlier. We just crossed that."

"Wow," Thomas said.

"Well, we'd better continue," Freddy said. "Let's go!"

So they continued on the path to Mount Tambox.

About ten minutes later, Thomas heard flapping wings, and dozens of Baranas swooped in. "After days of searching, we have finally found you naughty kids!" cackled their leader.

"Baranas!" said Freddy. "Run!"

"Ha ha ha!" cackled the leader. "You cannot escape that easily!"

The Baranas started breathing fire and shooting slime at them. Thomas tried to sprint away, but he wasn't fast enough. A glob of slime glued his foot to the ground. He tried to break free, but it was no use. This slime hardened into a rock.

Thomas frantically looked around and saw the others weren't having any luck, either. Mikey and Austin were glued to the ground with slime. And Freddy was watching the whole ordeal with a smile on his face. The Baranas weren't attacking him either.

One Barana was breathing fire at Austin. *Austin!* thought Thomas. His heart skipped a beat. But he couldn't do anything to save him.

A green Barana with a yellow eye swooped up behind Thomas. As he looked behind him, Thomas only caught a glimpse of the Barana as it surrounded him in flames. Thomas desperately tried to break free of the slime on his foot, pounding the slime with his hand, but it was no use. All he did was make his fist hurt.

The flames closed in around him. He slammed his free foot against the slime-rock. He could see nothing but searing hot flames.

But he heard one thing. He heard Freddy saying, "I have brought the children to you. Now I would like to receive my payment."

Then everything went dark.

Part Two

A Journey of Perils

CHAPTER SEVEN

The first thing Thomas registered when he regained consciousness was that he was cold. Freezing. The ground was hard, too. Was he under the overhang where he had slept the night before? It sure felt like it.

Thomas opened his eyes. He saw a rock wall. But it was smoother than the walls of the overhang. Where was he?

Then he saw the bars. He was in a cage! "What am I doing in a cage?" he said.

"I have no idea," Austin replied. He was in a cage in front of him. Looking around, he realized he was in one cell in an entire hallway of cages! The cages didn't seem to end.

"Where are we?" said Thomas.

"The Barana fortress, I think," Austin answered. "I saw a Barana earlier."

Barana. Barana fortress. Slowly, everything came back to Thomas. Where were the other kids? Where was Freddy?

"Thomas the Train! You survived!" came Mikey's voice.

"Hey, it's Thomas!" said Billy.

"You're alive!" said Thomas. He was relieved to see and hear Billy again.

"We were captured by turkeys!" said Billy.

"We have to escape!" said Marigold.

"Yeah, duh," scoffed Jane. "Of course we do!"

Thomas was happy that everyone was alive, but Marigold was right. They had to get out. But how?

Thomas sat down and stared at the rock wall. Now that he looked closely, he saw on the wall a carving of a Barana, except its tentacle was some sort of serpent.

"Guys?" Thomas asked. "Are there carvings on the walls in your cages?"

"Yes," Austin replied.

"Mine is a snake with a turkey on top!" said Billy.

"There are carvings over here in our cages," said Jane.

Hmm, Thomas thought. *That's weird.* He pressed the eye of the Barana. A secret passage opened up. "Press the eye of the Barana!" he yelled.

Next thing he knew, everyone was in the secret passage, and the doors were closed. "And what do we do now?" Jane asked.

Marigold had found something. "Hey!" she called. "There's a door that says dynamite storage over here!"

Everyone ran over, and Thomas pulled the door open. "Let's blow this place to bits!" Austin said.

Everyone grabbed some dynamite. On the side of the door, Thomas noticed matches and a matchbox. He grabbed one and lit it. Everyone dumped the dynamite in one of the cages. Thomas dropped the match into the pile of dynamite. "Take cover!" he yelled.

Everyone got down on the ground of the secret passage as the door to the cage closed. And then, *BOOM!*

Next thing he knew, Thomas was buried in rubble. He wasn't sure if anyone else was conscious. He hoped he wasn't the only one who survived the explosion.

"Guys?" he called, pushing a piece of stone off his back.

"Thomas!" said Billy, emerging from the rubble. Like Thomas, stony dust covered his hair.

"You're alive!" said Thomas.

"Yeah!" said Billy.

Pretty soon, Thomas discovered that everyone had survived. That was lucky. They needed to get to Mount Tambox.

The kids started on a nearby path. Thomas didn't know how far away they were from Mount Tambox. Still, he assumed that if they followed a path, it would eventually lead to a town where they could get directions to Mount Tambox.

All he knew was they were on their own now.

Pretty soon, they came across a bunch of Baranas, as well as Freddy, speaking with a Barana on a huge silver chair.

"Freddy?" Austin asked.

"Freddy...talking to Baranas?" Marigold said.

Then Thomas got it. "He must be working for the Baranas."

Everyone gaped. "Thomas is right, though," Mikey said. "Freddy said he led us to the Baranas, and he wanted his payment."

"Let's get him," Austin said.

"Shhh!" whispered Thomas. "Hide behind this vine. We can find out what they're up to."

The kids hid behind a large vine and listened to the Baranas. The one on the chair had a crown on its head, and Thomas assumed it was their king.

"Now that our fortress is gone, we must rebuild it," the Barana said. "Luckily, all of our captured children have survived, but six escaped the explosion."

"Yeah! It stinks!" hollered a Barana near the back.

"SILENCE!" orders King Barana. "We must rebuild our fortress. But we will not transform the children unless we have captured the escaped children."

Transform? thought Thomas. *What are they gonna do to us? And what do they mean by the other children?*

"But once we transform the children from the clashroom into ferocious lava monsters, we will be unstoppable! We will take over every universe like we did the first three!" said King Barana. The other Baranas cheered.

But Freddy didn't. "Why is Freddy the Frog not cheering?" Billy asked.

"Freddy the Frog?" muttered Mikey. "Really?"

"Freddy the Frog!" Billy repeated. "It makes sense, Mikey the Marker!"

"I am *not* a marker," Mikey hissed.

"And now," King Barana continued. "Freddy will die. He is of no further use to me."

Freddy's eyes went wide. "It was you!" he screamed. "You enslaved my universe!"

Freddy went into a fighting stance. But he was surrounded. He tried to run, but the Baranas slimed him to the ground. He struggled to get free.

The Baranas cackled as they flew away, carrying a struggling Freddy. Thomas heard one yell, "How will we choose which way to kill you?"

Thomas could only stare, horrified, as the Baranas flew out of sight. Then the kids all walked out of the bushes.

"They're gonna turn us into lava monsters!" Austin whispered.

"Not if they don't catch us," Mikey said. "We should steer clear of them."

"But they're gonna send their troops all overlooking for us," countered Marigold. "They're gonna catch us eventually."

"Not if we get out of this weird universe in general," said Jane. "We could just go home, and then they'll never catch us."

"But then they'll just activate the clashroom again!" protested Thomas. "We need to stop them somehow. And shouldn't we rescue Freddy?"

"No," Mikey said. "There's no way we can catch them, and all he did was lead us into Barana traps."

"Because they lied to him!" Austin protested.

"I'm afraid Mikey's right," Marigold said. "There's no way we can catch the Baranas. We don't know where they're going, and it's not like any of us can fly."

"We're going to have to stop them somehow," said Thomas. "They're going to take over the multiverse."

"Yeah," Austin agreed. "We can't just let them do that."

"How will we stop them?" Mikey asked. "We're just six kids who didn't even come here on purpose. Plus, four of us are nothing but airheads. Well, three of us. One of us is a train."

Austin slapped Mikey in the face. "Shut up," he said.

"We have to be cool kids and stop the turkeys!" Billy said.

"Sssh!" Jane hissed. "The Baranas might hear us! They could still be nearby!"

"Plus, they're Baranas, not turkeys," said Marigold.

"Turkeys!" said Billy.

"Baranas," Marigold corrected.

"Turkeys!" insisted Billy.

"Baranas," corrected Austin.

"Tur-" Mikey covered Billy's mouth.

"Shut up!" Mikey hissed through gritted teeth. "You wouldn't want any Baranas to hear us!"

"Anyway..." continued Thomas. "We need to stop the Baranas somehow."

"How?" Jane asked. But then, at that moment, a piece of paper fluttered to the ground.

"Huh? What's that?" asked Austin, picking up the piece of paper.

Thomas looked at the piece of paper over Austin's shoulder.

"It's a note!" he said.

"Why did a note fall from the sky?" asked Marigold.

"Maybe it has directions to Mount Tambox!" said Austin excitedly.

"Maybe," Thomas said. The note said:

If you have received this note, you are hopefully the last six kids that the Baranas are searching for. Once they capture you, they will turn you and 94 more kids into lava monsters to take over the multiverse.

For you to stop this, you must find The Jewel of Order. Once you have the Jewel of Order, King Barana will be capable of dying. Without it, he is immortal.

You must follow clues that will eventually lead you to the Jewel of Order. I'm afraid I can't tell you where it is right away because the Baranas may decipher it.

Here is your first clue: The relros protect it. Deep in the jungle. They could give you gelro, or give you the clue…

Your quest is no longer to get to the Universe Transporter. You must get the Jewel of Order.

Thomas read the note over and over again. "What?" he muttered.

"What? I can't hear you Thomas," Austin said.

Thomas showed Austin the note. The other kids read it over his shoulder.

"Wait, so we don't have to get to the Universe Transporter anymore?" Jane said.

"Yeah!" said Mikey. "We have to get this 'Jewel of Order'!" He did finger quotes when he said, "Jewel of Order."

"Yeah, and what the heck is a relro?" asked Thomas.

"And what's gelro? Is it bad?" said Austin.

"Duh!" Mikey said. "Of course, it's bad!"

"Okay, okay," muttered Austin.

At that moment, a horse was riding by, this time on a woman. The horse spotted the children.

"Horsey!" said Billy happily.

Ignoring Billy, Thomas started to speak. "Hi. Do you know what relros are?"

"Not from here, are you?" said the horse. "I figured, since you're humans and standing upright. I can tell you what relros are as soon as I get you to my house safely. You're the last kids the Baranas need."

"How do you know that?" asked Marigold.

"I'll tell you when we get to my house. We can't talk about it in the open. C'mon, hop on my human, and I'll tell you everything."

As they rode to the horse's house, Thomas thought about how weird it was that they were riding on a woman. The woman didn't even seem to mind that so many people were crammed on her.

A little while later, they got to the horse's house. It was a small house, but a nice one. When they got in, the horse invited them to sit at a table.

"Now that we're in safety, I can tell you about how I know about the Baranas," said the horse.

"Yes, please tell us," said Thomas.

"Okay," said the horse. "The thing is, I'm a secret agent. I have been spying on the Baranas to see what they're up to. You see, they've captured kids from the clash-"

"Um, we know," interrupted Mikey.

"Really?" asked the horse. "How do you know?"

Thomas told her about how they blew up the Baranas' fortress, then overheard them talking about their plan. They even told her about Freddy.

"Geez, right there in the open?" said the horse. "Guess they're not as secretive as I thought."

"Weren't you gonna tell us about relros?" said Mikey.

"Oh yes. I can tell you what a relro is. A relro is one of the most dangerous animals in this universe. They have poisonous bites, and the poison in the bites is called gelro." she said.

Then she added hastily, "Oh! I never even gave you a proper introduction! I'm so sorry. My name is Samantha. What are your names?"

The kids introduced themselves, and then Samantha said, "How about I can give you kids a bite to eat? Then I can give you more animal lessons."

"Yummy tacos?" asked Billy.

"Sorry, I don't have tacos, but I do have yorga goo," said Samantha.

Samantha served them each a bowl of yorga goo. Then she got started on their lesson.

Samantha told them about zoobaquels, and they were surprised to learn that there were basic ones and advanced ones. Basic ones acted like monkeys, while advanced ones had hidden civilizations and technology the horses didn't even have.

They also learned about faropas. The shopkeeper had been eaten by one, but they were nice if you gave them berries. They learned about furtigos, which were like vicious bears. By the time the yorga goo was gone, the kids knew nearly everything there was to know about the strange animals in this universe.

"Earlier, we were trying to get to the Universe Transporter," Thomas told Samantha. "But then this...note fell from the sky, and now we have to get the Jewel of Order."

Samantha paused for a moment. "The Universe Transporter?"

"Yes," Thomas said. "On top of Mount Tambox?"

"Thomas, I don't think the Universe Transporter even exists," Samantha said. "And if it did, why would it be on top of a dangerous mountain like Mount Tambox?"

Another one of Freddy's tricks, Thomas thought, grimacing.

"May I see the note?" Samantha asked.

Thomas showed her the note, and she read it. Then she said, "Well, relros only live in a specific part of the jungle. I can give you a map."

She walked away and rummaged through a cabinet. Finally, she pulled out a map and handed it to Thomas.

"Yay!" yelled Billy. "Now we can kill the naughty turkeys!"

"Well, you kids had better be on your way. Those Baranas are powerful," Samantha warned.

The kids said bye to Samantha, walked out of the house, and embarked on their journey.

CHAPTER EIGHT

The kids found a path that led to the relro region, and they started following that. The trail led into a deeper part of the jungle. The purple vines grew very close together, blocking out most of the sunlight.

Soon, they heard something ahead on the trail, but they couldn't see what it was. "Um, wha-" Thomas was interrupted by a roar!

"Look!" said Billy. "A doggie!"

"Billy, I don't think that's a dog," Thomas warned nervously. "I think it's a furtigo!"

The furtigo looked horrifying. It was maybe 15 feet head to tail, had jet black fur, big purple eyes, sharp teeth, and a long, whiplash tail. In general, it looked like a massive, mutated bear.

But there was no time to think about mutated bears, because Billy was running towards the furtigo!

"Yay!" yelled Billy. "A furry tigo!"

"Billy no-" said Thomas.

But he was too late. Billy was already trying to cuddle the furtigo!

Unfortunately, the furtigo was a ferocious beast, not an affectionate dog. It bit Billy and then scratched him with its massive claws.

"Hey!" cried Billy. "He bit me, and scratched me!"

"Run for your lives!" Thomas screamed at Billy and the others.

The kids sprinted away. They got a head start, but the furtigo was catching up fast. Thomas' legs were burning. But he kept running.

The furtigo was much faster than the kids. It grabbed Thomas by the shirt and flung him aside like he was a toy. "Oof," he groaned.

Once his vision returned, Thomas realized the other kids were in crumpled heaps, too. He felt like his back was broken. His arm certainly was.

Eventually, the furtigo lost interest and wandered off, satisfied that the intruders wouldn't be in its territory again. But that was only after the kids were so weak, they couldn't move.

Thomas didn't try to drag himself to a safer place. He just lay there, gasping for air. *If only I didn't get sucked into the clashroom,* he thought. *If only I faked being sick that day or something, then I wouldn't be in this mess! Now I'm going to die, and it's all those stupid Baranas' faults!*

Then, out of the blue, Thomas started feeling tingly. Then, his wounds began to heal! "Huh?" he said, energy restored.

It seemed the same thing was happening to the others! "What's going on?" said Jane.

"I dunno, but I feel weird," said Mikey.

"So do I," said Austin. "I feel all tingly."

"I love furry tigos," sighed Billy.

"How?" Jane asked, incredulous. "A 'furry tigo' just attacked us!"

They all climbed up onto their feet. They continued on the path, following Samantha's map.

A little while later, the kids heard stomping. This was more than just one furtigo or faropa. This sounded like 100 of either. "A pack of furtigos?!" Thomas exclaimed, horrified.

Twelve baby furtigos came through the vines! Even though they were babies, they were huge! About the size of large dogs.

Billy smiled. "Puppies!"

Somehow, he successfully cuddled one. Then he leaped on it and started riding around! "I'm a cowbruh!"

Then more adults came. They all looked as ferocious as the first one.

"Uh..." mumbled Jane. "We should go."

Then something terrifying happened. The baby furtigos grabbed the other kids! "I'm gonna die!" screamed Austin.

But unexpectedly, the baby furtigos threw the kids onto their backs! Then, as they rode around with kids on their backs, Thomas' furtigo tossed him in the air!

"AAAAHHH!" Thomas screamed.

It seemed like Thomas was going to land on the hard ground, but instead, he landed back on the baby furtigo's back.

"AAAHH!" he screamed again. He tried to get off the furtigo, but it started dancing around again, which made dismounting nearly impossible.

Fortunately, the little furtigo liked passengers. It danced along with other baby furtigos, which had the other kids on their backs.

Thomas grabbed the baby furtigo's fur for dear life and gazed over at Billy, who was having the time of his life.

"It's a furry tigo party!" he said as he rode upon his furtigo.

"How is this even happening?!" yelled Marigold.

"No idea!" said Austin.

At that moment, Billy was flung into the air! "Wee!" yelled Billy as he flew through the air.

Then he miraculously came back down on the furtigo. "Yay!" he cheered.

"Why are the furtigos making us ride them?" asked Austin.

"No clue!" everyone else replied at the same time.

Eventually, the baby furtigos let the kids off their backs. "That was fun!" said Austin.

"Yeah!" said Marigold. "It was awesome!"

The kids continued on the path, happily talking to each other about the furtigo party. They were so distracted that they didn't notice a sign they passed that said: "Now entering relro region. Proceed with caution."

But when Thomas stopped talking and looked up, he did notice a difference. It was more humid here, and the vines didn't grow so close together anymore. Unlike earlier, when all the vines were purple, some of the vines were light blue here. Bushes with light green leaves sprouted up here, and in the distance, Thomas could hear a river flowing.

"Wow," said Austin, who had also finally looked up. "It's beautiful here."

"This stupid humidity is ruining my hair!" said Jane.

"I hate it here!" yelled Mikey. "I hate this stupid humidity! I can't even breathe!"

Why do they always look on the negative side? thought Thomas. *Sure, it's humid, but it's also beautiful! Why don't they realize that?*

They continued to walk on the path towards the running river in the distance. When they reached the river, they got a big surprise.

"This river has sparks coming off of it, just like that other river!" Austin said.

Thomas looked at the map. "It might be that same river that the hawk knocked me into earlier!" said Thomas.

"We need to find a relro," Austin said.

"Duh!" said Jane.

"I agree," said Marigold. "But how do we get the clue from a relro?"

"I don't know, as a matter of fact," said Thomas.

"Wow!" said Mikey. "Thomas the Train is smart enough to realize he doesn't know anything!"

"For your information, I do know stuff," said Thomas. "I just don't know how to get the relro to give us the clue."

A couple of minutes later, they spotted a relro! It had scales, a long tail, fangs with poison dripping from them, and sharp claws.

"Look, a relro!" said Marigold in a hushed tone.

But it was on the other side of the river. "It's on the other side of the river!" Austin said.

"Um...duh," said Mikey. "Of course, it's on the other side of the river. Do you think we're all as dumb as you are?"

"Shut up, Mikey," muttered Thomas. "The point is we need to get across somehow."

Mikey started to say something mean when Marigold covered his mouth. "Are you just determined to say something mean every time someone says something?"

"It's not my fault everyone here is stupid," said Mikey, pushing away Marigold's hand.

"Well, maybe you're the stupid one," said Austin.

"How can I be so stupid when you're even stupider?" Mikey asked.

"Why do you even-"

Austin was interrupted by Thomas. "Stop fighting. We need to get across that river."

But before Thomas could continue, the relro spotted them and launched across the river! It whacked its tail into Mikey! Mikey went flying into the vines.

"RUN!" Austin yelled. They all sprinted away from the relro.

But the relro was gaining on them. Thomas sped away, but the relro was fast. There was no way they could stay in front of it. "Everyone look for something to distract the relro!" he yelled.

Billy picked up a shiny rock. It looked like a palm-sized lump of silver. "Look!" he said. "Shiny rock shiny rock fetch!"

He threw the rock. The relro turned around and chased it. It caught it in its mouth and wandered back over.

The relro seemed a lot friendlier with the rock in its mouth. And cuter. It was wagging its long tail and attempting to smile with the stone in its mouth. Thomas was surprised Billy didn't try to cuddle it.

"Why does it like the rock so much?" Jane asked.

"I don't know," said Austin.

Soon, they found Mikey, who, thankfully, wasn't hurt badly.

"Did you get the clue?" he asked.

"No, but Billy found a shiny rock, and the relro likes it," said Marigold.

"Weird," said Mikey.

They went to the place where they found the relro. The rock was by its side, and in its mouth was a note! "I think that's the next clue!" said Thomas.

The relro gave Thomas the clue. "Thank you!" he said, forgetting the relro was an animal and not a human being.

But as if it understood, the relro picked the rock up and scampered off into the jungle.

CHAPTER NINE

"We have the next clue!" said Thomas.

"Well, duh," said Mikey. "Why do you always state the obvious, Thomas the Train?"

"Shut up," Thomas said, reading the clue.

Congratulations! You have found the next clue. You must hurry. The Baranas are everywhere, searching for you. If they catch you, you will not be able to escape. You must be brave enough to survive, or you will die, obviously.

Here is your clue: In a friendly taco place, you must avoid the chase. Eat five tacos at this place, and then accept the race.

"This is a strange clue," said Marigold, who was reading over Thomas' shoulder.

Thomas turned around to see that everyone had been reading the clue over his shoulder! "Hey!" he said.

"There's only one clue," Jane said.

"I want to eat the tacos!" said Billy.

"But we don't even know where the 'friendly taco place' is," said Austin.

Thomas turned the note over. "Go east," it read.

"Okay, but which way is east?" Thomas asked nobody in particular. He knew how to tell directions, but he had no idea which way was east. He didn't know the geography of this universe.

Marigold looked up at the sun. "Why are you looking at the sun?" muttered Mikey.

"It's that way," said Marigold, pointing left.

"What's that way?" said Mikey.

"East. Duh."

"Hey! I'm not the stupid one!"

"Well, which way's north?"

"Uh...that way?" guessed Mikey, pointing right.

"That's west," said Marigold. "Duh."

"Well, I'm not a nerd like you!"

"You just said I was stupid."

"Yeah," said Mikey, rolling his eyes.

"Am I a nerd or stupid? Make up your mind."

"Both, duh. Nerds ARE stupid."

"Uh huh."

"Come on guys, we need to find the ne-" Thomas was interrupted.

"Yeah, guys! I wanna eat tacos!" Billy yelled. The kids walked in the direction Marigold pointed.

Soon, they arrived at something weird. The vines had grown sparsely up until now, but now they'd come across a wall of them.

Austin pushed one vine aside. There was a pool of lava! The other vines burst into flames!

"RUN!" Thomas yelled.

Everyone ran back the way they came except Billy. "Ooh!" he said.

He took a few steps back, then ran and leaped onto a light blue vine! The vine began to squirt out a dark purple juice.

"Mmmm!" he said as he drank it.

Some of the juice dribbled down his chin and onto the lava. Then something amazing happened! The juice spread across the lava, making a dark purple basalt.

"Wow!" said Billy. The others came running back.

"The lava is gone!" said Austin.

"Well, duh," said Mikey.

"How did you do it?" asked Thomas, looking at Billy.

"I drank the juice in the viney-vineys!" explained Billy. He pointed to a cluster of blue vines nearby. "Try it!"

Thomas hesitated, then broke off a piece of the vine and drank the juice inside. It was delicious, like a melted lemon lollipop, with a hint of grape! "Yum!" he said.

"It's yummy!" said Billy. "Try, other kids!" He looked at the others expectantly.

Mikey grumbled but broke off a small piece. "This is actually quite good!" he said. The others tried the juice, and everyone loved it.

It could have been seconds or days until Thomas finally said, "We have to keep on going."

Everyone groaned, but they knew they had to go. They continued past the purple basalt and along the river. Thomas thought it was strange that sparks were coming out of the water. Electricity and water just didn't go together.

They continued along until they reached a sign that said. "Now leaving relro territory. You are safe now. Yay."

"O...kay..." said Thomas, reading the sign.

"So yeet!" Billy said.

"I doubt this taco place is near," Thomas said.

But it just so happened that they weren't safe at all! Hundreds of Baranas were swooping through the vines. "I, Commander Tentacle, order you to... ATTACK!" the leader growled.

All of the Baranas, Thomas couldn't count how many, started to attack the kids with fire and slime! The kids began to sprint away.

The Baranas could fly, though. They caught up to the kids fast. Thomas turned around, praying another random fireball would appear, but it didn't.

A Barana swooped in and shot slime straight at Thomas. He dove on the ground. Soon, all the other kids were on the ground.

The Baranas were closing in. Twenty feet...fifteen feet... ten feet...five feet...

CHAPTER TEN

"ROAAAAAAAAAAAAAAR!"

Thomas looked at the others, confused. That was until three furtigos leaped over them and began to swat at the Baranas.

"Furry tigos to the rescue!" Billy cheered.

Within minutes, all the Baranas were dead, except for Commander Tentacle, who had fled.

"Okay, what just happened?" said Mikey.

"I do not know." Marigold said.

"Yay! The furry tigos saved us!" Billy said as the furtigos stomped off. But the last one stopped and licked Billy in the face. Billy licked it in return.

"Eww!" Jane squealed.

Now that the Baranas were gone, the kids could continue their journey. The path began to wind through the jungle. The kids followed it.

Soon they reached a fork in the path. A sign read, "Green Path, right. Blue Path, straight, Yellow Path, left."

"Which way should we go?" asked Marigold.

"I don't know," replied Thomas. "Let's just go on Blue Path."

"What makes you so smart, Thomas the Train?" asked Mikey. "Why shouldn't we take Yellow Path?"

"Do you have a better way to choose a direction?" Marigold asked.

Mikey grumbled, but the kids started down the trail.

"Wait!" said Austin. "Look! The back of the sign says Green path goes to Walkinville, home to the best tacos in history!"

"You're right!" Thomas said. "Let's follow Green Path!"

"Duh!" said Mikey. "I saw that a loooong time ago, but I just wanted to prove you were stupid, Thomas the Train!"

"Okay," said Marigold. "Then why did you say we should take the *yellow* path?"

"Well... I mean... um... like... um..." Mikey stuttered.

"Yeah," said Austin.

The kids started to walk down the Green Path. Night was beginning to fall. "We better get to Walkinville soon," said Thomas. "I can't see very well."

Soon, it was almost pitch black. "Whoa!" Thomas said, stumbling on a rock. It seemed nobody else could see either. Everyone was tripping over stuff.

Thomas was the first to notice the lights after an hour of stumbling through the dark. "Look!" he said.

Everyone turned to look where Thomas was pointing through the dark. "Walkinville woot!" Billy sang.

They all walked into the town. "Woohoo!" Marigold yelled. They turned a corner and saw a building with a sign that said, "WALKINVILLE TACOS! Come and Enjoy 24/7!"

"Tacos!" Billy yelled, sprinting into the building.

Thomas followed Billy inside the building, not giving a glance to the windows. But inside the building was not what Thomas had expected.

Instead of happy families crowded around tables and the delicious smell of tacos, Thomas just saw an empty room and a counter.

"Um...what?" asked Austin. "Where's the taco place?"

Then they heard a cackling laugh. Baranas were surrounding them! "Aaaah!" said Jane.

King Barana flew in too. "Looks like you fell into our little trap. I am King Barana, and you are ours," he said.

The Baranas lunged at the kids, trying to grab them with their slimy tentacles. Thomas leaped onto a table and jumped onto the counter before falling on his face. He groaned, trying to crawl into the back room.

He got up and ran through the curtains, only to find almost a hundred more Baranas. "Other way! Other way!" he said.

He sprinted back through the curtains and punched a Barana in the face. It was stunned, and he grabbed its tentacle, spinning in a circle. The Barana he had caught whacked all the Baranas attacking Thomas.

Thomas bolted for the door. More Baranas were coming at him. He turned the doorknob, but it hardly budged. "C'mon, c'mon!" Thomas said, turning the doorknob frantically. But it was no use. The door was locked.

The Baranas were closing in around him. "Whoa!" he yelped. Thomas was exhausted, but if he didn't do something, he would be dead. So, he grabbed a Barana by its tentacle and swung it like a baseball bat, knocking the other Baranas to the ground. Then he sprinted towards the other kids.

"What will we do now?" asked Marigold.

"I don't know!" said Thomas.

"You got us into this mess," said Mikey. "Now you gotta get us out!"

The Baranas had shifted from just trying to grab them to shooting their slime, trying to glue them to the spot. Thomas again grabbed two Baranas and spun in a circle. Soon, the two Baranas were covered entirely in rock-hard slime. Thomas flung them straight through the other Baranas and then repeated the process. But the Baranas were slowly coming closer.

"We need to do something!" said Thomas. "We can't just dodge forever!"

"But what will we do?" said Austin. "Those crazy Baranas have a bunch of powers, and we're just six kids who got here by accident!"

Everyone ran and hid behind the counter. "We're so doomed. We are very, very doomed" Thomas said.

The Baranas swooped in, reaching out with their tentacles. The kids scooted away, only to find more Baranas. One reached out for Thomas…

The Barana's tentacle was only one inch away when the counter began to levitate. Everyone, including the Baranas, turned. Marigold was looking a little green. Thomas expected it was just from the craziness of it all.

The counter began spinning and moving around, flinging maybe a hundred Baranas into the walls. The counter then fell with a crash.

"The turkeys are dead!" Billy said.

"How did that counter do that?" asked Thomas.

"I dunno," said Marigold. "That was weird."

Although many Baranas had been knocked out by the levitating counter, lots of Baranas were still alive. They started firing slime at the six kids.

The Baranas began to close in on the kids. Next thing Thomas knew, he and the others were glued to the floor. The Baranas were reaching out with their tentacles now, only inches away.

Thomas heard a CRASH! He looked around just in time to see a colossal faropa that looked more than fifteen feet tall. It smashed almost every Barana before coming over to Thomas.

Thomas could feel his face slick with sweat. Was the faropa going to eat him? He watched as the faropa smashed the rock-hard slime Thomas had thought indestructible like glass.

A Barana swooped down and breathed fire at the unsuspecting faropa. The faropa turned around and threw the Barana into a wall before releasing everyone else.

"Can we go now?" Jane asked cautiously.

The faropa looked at Jane curiously. Jane flinched, but the faropa didn't attack. Well, it did, but it attacked the remaining Baranas. Within minutes, every Barana except for King Barana was dead.

"You may have defeated my army this time, but not me!" cried King Barana.

Thomas wanted to tell him that it wasn't him but a faropa that had helped them, but King Barana had already flown off into the sky.

Thomas realized that the door to the fake taco place was unlocked, so they exited through that. He was relieved that the whole ordeal was over.

"So now what?" said Mikey. "The taco place we found was fake, so we have no idea where the real place is!"

"I'm pretty sure we still have to go east," said Thomas.

"Yeah, whoever is writing these clues is obviously on our side," said Austin, then paused. "Unless they're trying to kill us, but I don't think that's the case."

"Well, the sooner we find that jewel of whatever, the sooner we get home," Mikey said. "So let's go!" They took off.

Thomas still couldn't believe he was in another universe. Just earlier that week, he had thought alternate universes couldn't exist.

But yet, here he was, walking down a path with five of his classmates in an alternate universe. Weirder yet, there were more universes out there, and they were doomed unless Thomas and his friends got the Jewel of Order.

He couldn't believe it.

"I just hope this taco place is close," said Thomas. "Like around the corner or something."

"The Baranas wouldn't put a fake taco place right by the real deal," Jane said.

"Yeah, Thomas the Train, you're so dumb you can't even realize that," said Mikey.

"Look, would you guys just stop?" Thomas pleaded. "You're really getting on my nerves."

"Yeah, stop bullying us," agreed Austin. "You're being jerks."

"Nobody likes dummy dumb bullies!" Billy declared.

"Shut up," said Jane. "Just shut up."

"Yeah, I don't need you dummies to boss me around!" said Mikey.

"Seriously?" said Marigold.

Mikey was about to say something else, but then a thundering boom shook the ground. "Whoa!" said Thomas.

Thomas was about to say something when something horrifying happened. The ground opened up, and lava began to pour out! The kids screamed.

The lava was flowing fast. Thomas barely even heard himself screaming as he sprinted as fast as his legs would allow him. The lava was speeding up.

Austin, who was in front, slowed down. "Canyon!" he warned. Everyone skidded to a halt.

"Keep running!" Marigold screamed.

Everyone had a delayed response, but they all looked at the lava and sprinted towards the canyon. And it was a massive canyon.

As Thomas sprinted forward, he noticed that six vines were hanging over the canyon. Everyone else saw too. "We'll have to jump and grab those vines!" Marigold yelled.

"Yeah!" Austin agreed. "But one of them is a little too far out!"

Austin was right. Five of the vines were hard but not impossible jumps. The sixth, though, was a couple of feet further.

Thomas really wanted to jump for the closer ones.

"He really wished it was Mikey or Jane who would jump for the far ones. But they never would. They were too selfish. Thomas really wanted to jump for a close one.

But what about Austin? Marigold? Billy? They were his friends. He wanted them to live. Be he wanted to live too! Him, or his friends. Who would it be?"

At that moment, he made his decision. "I'll take the far one!" he screamed.

"But...you're not going to make it!" yelled Austin.

"Just listen!" Thomas commanded.

Before they could change their minds, everyone leaped. Thomas heard himself screaming.

Was he going to make it? The vine was about eight feet from the cliff edge. Thomas was pretty sure only professional long jumpers could jump that far. But there was no turning back now. He was already flying through the air. Thomas suddenly wished he had given second thoughts to this feat before leaping out to grab the vine.

Thomas saw that his friends had grabbed onto the vines that were only about three feet from the cliff. *Good, they survived,* Thomas thought. *But will I?*

The vine was coming closer. Thomas reached out to grab the vine... but instead held open air.

I jumped too far. How did I jump too far?

But there was no time to worry about that because Thomas was falling.

CHAPTER ELEVEN

Thomas screamed. The vine was now hundreds of feet away. He looked down. The canyon went down for miles. He could barely make out the glowing lava at the bottom. He could only imagine what else lay at the bottom of the chasm. *Soon enough,* he thought, *it'll be my bones.*

He was halfway across the chasm when he got the idea. If he could just make it far enough...

Thomas could see the glowing lava much better now. He was falling too fast! But he just had to make it a few more feet...

He reached out and grabbed onto a ledge on the rock wall. He had crossed the entire canyon. Now, he just had to rock climb what seemed like a mile. *At least I'm alive,* he thought.

He heaved himself onto the ledge, which was about a foot wide. He looked up. Lucky for Thomas, the canyon wall was jagged. He reached up and grabbed a small rock sticking out of the cliff and pulled his foot up into a crack. And so the climb began.

Thomas started taking rock-climbing lessons in 3rd grade and had continued doing them. Three years of rock-climbing lessons were undoubtedly going to be helpful. He grabbed another ledge and pulled his foot up onto a small rock sticking out of the cliff face.

A gust of wind blew past Thomas' back. *Don't look down,* he reminded himself, grabbing another handhold.

But, even after three years of rock climbing, he made the mistake of looking down. His stomach dropped. It seemed he was ten thousand miles above the bottom of the canyon, where there was boiling lava waiting for him. If he simply slipped, it would be his doom.

No, he thought. *Concentrate on climbing.* He placed his feet onto some rocks, feeling a lot more scared.

Another sudden gust of wind blew. Thomas felt a jolt in his stomach. But he didn't fall off. He breathed a sigh of relief and kept going.

It only took about 30 minutes of climbing for Thomas to get tired. His arms ached. He looked up again and saw a ledge he could stand on without having to grab onto something. He reached up for a handhold but found none. He would have to jump and grab the ledge.

Thomas leaped up and managed to grab on with one hand. He grabbed on with his other hand and hauled himself onto the ledge.

He only rested for about 10 minutes. Then he grabbed a small rock with both hands and stuck his foot in a small crack in the rock. There seemed to be lots of good handholds for the next 100 feet of climbing.

Thomas was about 500 feet from the top when he slipped. He had been trying to grab a rock but had pulled his foot up too early. He managed to grab onto the rock with one hand, but it was a lousy handhold. He desperately tried to grab on with his other hand.

He was hanging by one, slipping hand. He clawed at the ledge with his free hand. He was about to fall when his hand latched on to a good handhold. He pulled himself up and sighed with relief. That was a close call!

Thomas was nearly to the top when he heard his name. It was quiet at first, but as he climbed, it got louder and louder. "Thomas! Thomas! Thomas! Thomas!"

It was his friends cheering him on! Thomas smiled but wondered how they were seeing him from all the way over there.

As Thomas got closer and closer to the top, he noticed that the voices weren't coming from the middle of the canyon where the vines were, but from the cliff edge! His friends had somehow made it across!

Thomas was exhausted. He almost fell asleep, almost gave up, but then he heard his friends chanting again. *So close!* he thought.

Five minutes later, Thomas' hand felt the cool grass on this side of the canyon.

Billy and Marigold grabbed Thomas and pulled him onto the grass. In maybe two minutes, he was asleep.

"They have escaped!" King Barana roared.

"Sir, what shall I do?" Commander Tentacle asked.

"We must find the Jewel of Order before them," King Barana growled.

"But why do *we* want the jewel?" asked Commander Slimio. "It makes *you* mortal if they have–"

"To destroy it," King Barana growled. "And if you don't stop asking questions, you'll be destroyed too!"

Commander Slimio did not say another word. "So, how do we get it before them?" Commander Tentacle asked.

"You must set a trap."

Thomas awoke to Billy tapping on his shoulder. "Thomas the Tomato isn't dead!" Billy announced.

"I'm not a tomato," mumbled Thomas.

"That's right," said Mikey. "He's a train!"

"I'm a human being!" said Thomas.

"Are you Thomas the Tractor?" Billy asked.

"No," Thomas replied.

"Are you Thomas the Tornado?"

"No!"

"Are you Thomas the Thomas?"

"Sure."

"I will call you Thomas!" Billy said.

"Thank you," Thomas replied, exasperated.

Austin helped Thomas up, and they continued walking east. After about 30 minutes, Thomas saw vines in the distance. It seemed they would be traveling through a forest again.

As they got closer, Thomas noticed this forest was different from the others. There were only a few vines scattered around, but many more trees. And the trees were strange. Their trunks were purple with tiny red needles sticking out of them, and they had bright blue leaves that extended out hundreds of feet away from the tree. The soil on the ground also had a yellow tint to it.

Weird, thought Thomas.

"This forest is so weird," said Jane.

"Yeah!" agreed Marigold. "But also kind ofcool."

"Well, duh. This is another universe," said Mikey. "Everything is weird here."

"Especially all the weird disaster things," Marigold said.

One of the leaves floated down onto the ground. Billy picked it up. It made a crunching noise, and Thomas noticed it was thick. Very thick, in fact, maybe an inch. A sweet smell drifted from it. It smelled like a mint Oreo.

"That smells really good!" Jane said.

"Totally!" Marigold said. "They should make this into some type of breath mint or perfume!"

The kids continued down a beaten path through the strange, yet beautiful forest. They marveled at all the strange plants and creatures. Thomas watched as what looked like an oversized green chipmunk scurried across the path and into a dark purple bush with white thorns.

Billy pointed out an animal that looked like a cat with gold and blue stripes digging a den under a rock. Thomas wished he had a camera to take pictures of all the beautiful creatures and scenery here.

Thomas' mind wandered back to the taco place, which, surprisingly, he hadn't thought about for quite some time. He grabbed the crumpled clue from his pocket.

In a friendly taco place, you must avoid the chase. Eat five tacos at this place, and then accept the race.

"Hopefully the taco place is around here somewhere," said Thomas.

The ground began to shake. Thomas could feel the rumbling all the way in his bones. "Guys," Austin warned. "I think this is an earthquake! Cover your head!"

Everyone jumped on the ground and put their hands over their heads. The ground shook violently and wasn't showing any sign of slowing down. Thomas looked further down the path and noticed an open plain in just a few minutes' run.

"Everyone, run for the plain!" Marigold yelled.

Thomas half expected Mikey to return some mean remark, but he guessed Mikey was too distracted trying not to die. Everyone sprinted for the plain. The ground was shaking harder and harder.

Thomas was only 30 feet away from the plain when he noticed the tree trunk heading straight for his head.

CHAPTER TWELVE

Thomas stared in horror as the tree came down. He willed his limbs to move, but he couldn't. He was too horrified.

"MOVE THOMAS!" Austin screamed.

Thomas couldn't. All he could do was stare at the tree that was going to crush him in seconds.

The tree was only inches away from Thomas' head when Billy dove into him, sending them both flying into a thorny bush. The tree hit the ground just inches from Thomas and Billy with a ground-shaking *CRASH!*

For a second, everything was silent. Even the earthquake stopped. And then Billy said, "I did it!"

"Thanks, Billy!" Thomas said. "I owe my life to you. Literally."

"It's okay!" Billy replied.

Thomas' stomach growled. He hadn't eaten anything since... who knows when. A taco or five sounded good right now.

Thomas climbed out of the bush and walked into the plain. As soon as he walked out of the forest, he noticed the flashing sign in the fading light of day reading, "TONY'S TERRIFIC TACOS! NOW OPEN!"

"The taco place!" said Thomas. "We should try and get there before nightfall!

Billy sprinted ahead, excited to get some tacos. Everyone else followed, and the next thing they knew, they had arrived at the taco place.

They went into the taco store. The amazing smell of chicken tacos wafted into Thomas' nose. He went up to the counter, only to realize they had no money! Luckily, he noticed the sign that said, "Free tacos on the first of every month!" As well as the calendar that had different month names but still said *Yolader 1st*.

Thomas ordered 18 tacos, three per person. In minutes, they were ready. "Chow down!" he said, bringing the tacos to the table.

Billy was the first one to reach in to grab a shredded beef taco. He bit in, green chile dribbling down his chin onto his napkin. "Mmmmmm!" he said through a bite.

Everyone enjoyed some tacos. Thomas was surprised that tacos tasted so typical and delicious in this universe. But still, these were the best tacos *ever.*

After they finished eating, a waiter came over and handed them a paper. It read, "If you order 15 tacos or more, you can enter this race and choose from a selection of prizes if you win!"

Thomas showed the others, and they ultimately decided this must be the race they have to enter to get the clue. The waiter came back and asked if they would enter the race. They did.

The race would start in the morning, so all the kids settled down in their sleeping bags just outside the town.

The next morning, the kids walked to the racing course, excited to see what they would be racing on. But it wasn't a typical race. They had to ride around on a scooter that floated, except they had to wear special white gloves. The gloves had buttons to turn, speed up, slow down, and go up or down. As they raced on the scooter things, they would have to dodge obstacles and other players. The first person to the finish won.

As they were putting on their helmets and gloves at the starting line, Mikey said, "We're not going to win this. We've never used these things before."

"We *have* to win this," said Thomas. "To save the multiverse."

There were seven other contestants that they were racing against. They were all lined up at the starting line already, and it seemed like they knew how to use these things. Nobody paid any mind to Thomas and his friends. They probably thought they would get crushed five minutes in. Thomas didn't know whether they were right or wrong.

But Thomas had no time to worry because he heard a bang, and the race began. He pressed hard on the acceleration and zoomed forward. He checked the small speedometer on his glove: 47 miles per hour.

Thomas noticed a massive sandstone tower in front of him and swerved left, dodging the building by inches. He checked his glove. He was in 5th place!

He looked in front and saw Billy fly off of a ramp over top of some purple alien. Billy pressed down on the down button on his glove right in front of the purple alien. The purple alien narrowly avoided Billy but crashed into some other contestant.

Thomas noticed he had jumped to 4th place. He sped up, trying to gain on some more contestants. He looked up just in time to see a massive stone tower in front of him. He jammed the up button and narrowly avoided blowing himself up. He needed to focus on the race!

He crested the top of the tower and zoomed back down. He leveled out about a foot off the ground and swerved around another tower. He was already getting the hang of this thing.

But right behind the tower, there was another. Thomas jammed on the left button, avoiding the stone tower by inches.

The next obstacle was a large wall with a ramp. You had to climb the ramp and either go over the wall or go down through a small hole in the wall and gain one boost charge. Thomas chose the latter.

Thomas zoomed up the ramp before swerving down and flying through the hole, narrowly avoiding an explosion.

Thomas noticed that a small button lit up on his glove. It said 1 boost charge. Thomas reached a maximum acceleration of 50 miles an hour. He lined his flying scooter in a path that would take him between any obstacles.

He pressed hard on the boost button, and his speed immediately jumped to 75 miles per hour. Thomas heard a chime as he jumped from 4th to 3rd to 2nd and all the way to 1st. Then his boost stopped.

Thomas saw that Austin, Billy, and Mikey were just behind him. Thomas smiled, but then his foot slipped off his flying scooter. He struggled to regain balance.

Luckily, he did, just in time to swerve around another tower. He was still in first, but other contestants were catching up fast.

Thomas looked back and saw that Jane and Marigold's scooters had been cut in half! They were both rolling through the sand. Another purple alien was speeding forward with some kind of blade coming out of his scooter! *Cheater!* Thomas thought.

Thomas avoided more obstacles as the flying got harder and harder. Mikey and Austin both got their scooters cut by the cheating alien and so did the other contestants that weren't one of the kids. Only Billy, Thomas, and the cheater were left.

Next thing Thomas knew, though, Billy's scooter was cut, and the cheater was gaining on Thomas. He swerved to the far right to dodge the cheater. The cheater zoomed into first place.

Thomas swerved around a tower. As soon as he made it around, another tower came into view. Thomas jammed on the right button, narrowly avoiding the tower. Thomas swerved left and right over and over. The cheater was getting further and further ahead.

The final obstacle was approaching. You either leaped over the stone wall after going up a ramp or went between the ramps and got a boost. Then you either tried to go over the wall or go between a crack in it that could probably fit an inch on either side of your scooter.

Thomas only had one way to win. He zoomed straight between the ramps and slammed hard on the boost button. The wall came rushing up. Thomas lined up his scooter and soared through the crack!

He and the cheater were tied now. The blades on the cheater's scooter opened up. Thomas slammed his scooter into the cheater's. The cheater flipped off his scooter just as Thomas crossed the finish line. Thomas had won!

A normal human came up and presented Thomas with his prize options. He chose a folded piece of paper that was probably the clue.

As the prize presenter walked away, all Thomas' friends ran up. Thomas was hit by a barrage of questions.

"How did you beat the cheater?"

"How did you fit in that gap?"

"How did you not fall off the scooter?"

Thomas answered them one by one. "I had to crash into the cheater to win. It was crazy! I have no idea how I fit the gap. I just did. All I did was hold my balance!"

"That was so cool!" Billy said.

Thomas showed everyone the clue once they left the racing course.

Great work! You only need to find four more clues until you find The Jewel of Order. The Baranas are searching vigorously for you. You are the last six kids they need to complete their army and take over the multiverse. Be careful and work together to survive.

Here is your next clue: In a sticky tunnel, you must avoid the pummel. Ride through the funnel while dodging the rubble and pursue your next clue.

"Avoid the pummel?" Austin said. "That can't be good."

"Well, *duh!*" Mikey said. "Do you *think* it would be good?"

"Yay!" said Billy. "We get to ride through a funnel!"

"While dodging the rubble," Jane said. "That can't be fun."

"But it's called a *fun*nel!" Billy protested. "It'll be fun!"

"But..." Thomas said. "Where is the tunnel?"

Thomas turned the clue over. The clues had stuff on the back before. Maybe it would again. Turns out, it did! It read: "Follow the southern path out of Walkinville. It'll be the first opening in the mountain."

Thomas showed the others, and they set out on their journey.

Chapter Thirteen

The kids had only been walking on the southern path out of Walkinville for about 30 minutes when they reached the mountain.

"The tunnel must be somewhere around here!" Thomas said.

"Hopefully, we won't have to go much further."

They didn't. Five minutes later, Thomas noticed a small opening in the mountain. There was a sign next to it that read:

"Danger! The sticky substance on these walls may attract you with its sweet smell, but if you touch it, you will be glued to this wall for eternity! We recommend that you do not enter. Exactly 0 people have ever returned from this cave! No worries, only 0 have entered! Don't get stuck."

"This has to be the sticky cave," said Mikey, who had been reading the sign over Thomas' shoulder.

"Why do you think so?" asked Thomas.

"Because it's deadly, duh," said Mikey.

Thomas kneeled down and looked at the opening. It looked barely big enough for a mouse, let alone a human. Thomas squeezed through the rocky opening. The tunnel was a little bit more spacious, but he still only had a few inches on either side of him.

Thomas called to the others. "Come on, guys!"

Billy squeezed through next, followed by Marigold, Jane, Austin, and Mikey. Thomas started crawling through the tunnel. It was tough not to touch the sticky stuff on the walls.

Thomas' arms started hurting after about 15 minutes. Crawling hurt more than he thought. Thomas looked ahead for any sign of the cave getting wider. Up ahead, there could be something. The tunnel seemed to grow enough that they could comfortably stand.

Turned out, it was further away than Thomas had thought. They had crawled for another 15 minutes, and it seemed they weren't any closer. "How long is this?" Austin whined. "My legs are cramping up."

"How am I supposed to know?" Thomas countered.

"You're not," Mikey answered. "You're too dumb to know how long this is."

Thomas' legs were cramping up too. His muscles ached, and he couldn't stretch, or he'd be glued to the tunnel for eternity. "I think this tunnel opens up a little further down," Thomas called.

There was a mix of grumbling and cheering. Austin said that it would just make it feel further. Marigold was excited she would be able to move around again.

When the tunnel finally did open up, everyone cheered. It was still a tunnel but was as wide as a cave now. The sticky stuff still lined the walls, though.

After everyone had climbed to their feet and stretched, they continued down the tunnel. All was peaceful until Thomas heard a click. "What was that?" he asked.

Before anyone could answer with "I don't know," rocks began raining from holes that had opened up in the roof of the cave! "Run!" Marigold yelled.

Everyone sprinted as rocks rained from the ceiling, jumping and dodging. A rock cracked across Thomas' head. He saw stars behind his eyes. Then someone pushed him, and he began running again.

Thomas saw that Marigold's arm was stuck under a rock. He ran over and heaved the rock off her arm, just in time to dive out of the way of a rock the size of his hand.

Thomas kept running. He paid attention to the holes in the ceiling, diving away from each one.

The tunnel was beginning to slope downward now. The rocks started to roll down the tunnel, piling on top of each other. Soon, the entire tunnel would be clogged!

Thomas sprinted forward, dodging rock after rock. Then he heard the rumble. It grew louder and louder. He looked back. A massive boulder was rolling through the tunnel. "Boulder!" Thomas screamed.

Everyone looked confused for a second until they saw the boulder. Then they ran. They ran as fast as they could. Thomas' head throbbed. Rocks pummeled him like hail. That's when he got it. This was the pummel!

Rocks rolled down the slope. Thomas could barely keep his footing as he sprinted forward. Billy got hit on the head with a rock. "Stars!" he said.

Thomas grabbed him and pulled him forward. "C'mon Billy!" he urged.

Billy ran forward. *Whew!* Thomas thought. The boulder was speeding down the slope, crushing or flinging all the rocks away. One of them hit Thomas in the back of the shin.

He tripped on a rolling rock the size of his head and went down. The stones started pulling him down. His head bonked against rock after rock after rock. He saw stars again, and they wouldn't go away.

Thomas groaned. A rock dropped on his arm. "Ow!" Thomas said in surprise.

Thomas flipped over and bumped into Austin, who fell on top of him. Their heads bonked, and they became a tangle of limbs. Austin's elbow hit Thomas' armpit, and he cried out in pain.

Thomas saw the boulder. It was zooming up to greet him. Someone screamed, maybe him. He didn't know. All he knew was that the boulder was about to crush him and Austin.

He tried to scramble to his feet but couldn't on the rolling rocks. He grabbed Austin and lifted himself, and pulled Austin up. "Come on, Austin!" he yelled.

Austin, startled, sprinted down the tunnel. Thomas ran after him. He looked for the place where the pummeling rocks would stop.

The rocks were coming down faster and bigger now. Every few seconds, a rock would hit Thomas. He could already feel his head swelling up.

Another rock hit Thomas on the head. His left eye began to swell shut, but he kept running. He saw that Marigold was on the ground now, and Jane had just crashed into Mikey, sending them both tumbling to the ground.

Thomas lifted Marigold just as a rock hit his arm. Marigold wasn't looking good. Her face was bruised, one of her arms seemed broken, and her leg was swollen up. "C'mon!" he wheezed, not having the strength to yell.

Mikey and Jane helped each other up before Thomas could, which was good because the boulder was gaining on them fast.

Thomas thought he saw something up ahead. Some kind of cliff or steep slope instead of the gradual one they were on.

Thomas heard a scream. He looked back. It was Austin! His hand was stuck in the substance on the walls. He was about to get crushed by the boulder!

CHAPTER

FOURTEEN

"Austin!" Thomas screamed.

Thomas tried to run back to help Austin, but the rolling rocks stopped him. All he could do was stand there and watch, helpless. The boulder was going to crush Austin in seconds.

The ground began to shake. Not just the rumble of the boulder, something bigger. Thomas reached out his hand like it would stretch and pull Austin back.

The ground shook harder and harder. And then...***BOOM!***

The place where the boulder had been exploded, destroying the boulder and disintegrating the sticky substance trapping Austin's arm.

Austin looked surprised at first but then started running. More rocks were rolling down the slope.

The cliff Thomas had noticed earlier was getting closer…closer...

Thomas leaped right into a funnel. Rocks were rolling down it, and he saw Mikey, Jane, Billy, and Marigold were sliding down it. Austin jumped in behind Thomas.

Thomas slid down the funnel leaping over rock after rock. He *needed* to get through the bottom before it clogged! "C'mon guys, we have to hurry!" he called to the others.

Everyone got up and started running down the funnel. A rock hit Thomas in the leg, and he tumbled down the funnel, banging his head on the smooth stone.

The bottom had almost clogged all the way up when Thomas and the others got down. "We're too late!" Austin said. "We'll have to move the rocks!"

The problem was that rocks were starting to pile up on top of the kids. "Move the rocks! Hurry!" Thomas said.

They lifted the rocks and threw them as far as they could onto the funnel, but rocks were starting to cover them. Thomas balled up, protecting his head.

Before he knew it, they were completely covered in stones. Thomas un-balled himself, shifting the rocks above him. The sound of rocks piling above them was muffled now.

Thomas started moving rocks, trying to unclog the tunnel before they ran out of oxygen. Billy got up and helped too.

"Austin?" Thomas asked. "You're good at air science, how much time do we have until we're out of oxygen?"

"About an hour," Austin groaned.

"Only an hour?!" Thomas repeated, starting to work faster. "Help us, guys!"

Everyone began moving rocks. They had a small air pocket, so they put the rocks in it.

Thomas' arms were aching. How many rocks would they have to move? Would they be able to fit them all?

Thomas didn't know, but he kept working. They had to get the clue. "Come on, Mikey! Help us out over here!" Thomas urged.

Mikey grumbled and picked up a rock. Thomas grabbed one and moved it aside. "Are we ever going to get out of here?" Marigold asked.

"Not if we don't work fast," Thomas replied.

"Will we die?" Billy asked.

"I sure hope not," Austin answered.

Thomas kept on moving rock after rock. The stones seemed endless. Were they ever going to get out?

Before he knew it, Thomas was gasping for air. The rocks went on and on. Thomas felt like giving up. There was no way out. It was a bottomless pit of rocks. They were doomed.

Thomas moved another rock aside, and some stones underneath it fell. "Huh?" he gasped.

Thomas stuck his arm through the rocks. He felt air. Air! They had reached the end of the funnel!

"Guys!" Thomas said, gasping for air. "I found the end of the funnel! Come quick!"

Thomas heard cheering. Then rocks moving as the kids made their way to Thomas.

Marigold stuck her arm through the rocks. "You're right, Thomas!" she said. "There's air!"

"I thought we were going to die!" said Austin.

"Me too," sighed Thomas.

Everyone crawled down the opening, and they came out in a giant golden room. It had a white pedestal in the center with a scroll placed atop it. They unraveled the scroll and read it.

Wow! You are brave to find this clue. There are only three clues left until you find The Jewel of Order. But you are in great danger. The Baranas are spread out all over the planet, searching for you. They won't stop until they find you. They even set up traps to get you in their clutches. Be careful!

Here is your next clue: In a Land of Emerald Hail, the clue will prevail. Follow the sound of the howling wolf and find your next clue by the obsidian gulf.

Thomas gave the clue to the others. "Emerald hail?" Austin asked. "That can't be good. And a gulf made of obsidian? Does that have something to do with the emerald hail?"

"We'll need to ask someone where the 'Land of Emerald Hail' is," Marigold said.

"Yeah, well, duh," Mikey said. "Me and Jane are not so dumb that people need to state the obvious, like you dummies!"

"Uhh, Mikey..." Austin chuckled. "The correct grammar is Jane and I, so..."

"So what, Grammar Police?" Mikey protested.

"So, we're not the dumb ones."

"Can we please just go find the clue so we can get out of this stupid place?" Jane interjected.

"How do we get out?" Austin asked.

"Maybe that?" Thomas replied, pointing to a stone button on the wall.

Mikey ran over and pressed it. The ground rumbled, and the ceiling above them began to slide away, revealing a long shaft. The room lurched upward and started its ascent.

It took about five minutes for the elevator room to reach the top, but it eventually did.

Everyone hopped off before the elevator room slid back down and became concealed again.

Thomas shivered. The wind was howling. He looked around. They were on the top of the mountain! Thomas saw a sign. It read: "Mt. Elocamba, 2nd tallest mountain in the known universe! Elevation: 37,084 feet above sea level."

He looked out across the landscape. He could see Walkinville nearby. He also saw another town far in the distance and something that seemed to be shining green. "Maybe that's the Land of Emerald Hail!" said Thomas, pointing to the green thing.

Austin looked over. "I sure hope so, that seems like a long walk, and there's nowhere closer."

The wind howled in Thomas' ear. "Man, it's cold up here," Marigold shuttered, looking at the sign.

"Can we just get down where it's warm?" Jane asked, shivering. "I'm in jean shorts and a tank top."

"How do we get down?" asked Austin. "Is there a trail?"

Everyone looked around on the big summit. It didn't take them long to find the beaten path covered in the gleaming blue snow of this universe. Austin called them over, and they began the long hike down.

CHAPTER FIFTEEN

Thomas was exhausted. They had been hiking down Mt. Elocamba for hours; he didn't know how many anymore.

The howling wind was still blowing, and it wasn't getting any warmer. Thomas felt like he had frostbite. A T-shirt and jeans weren't the clothes to hike down a cold mountain. *I wish I had my sweater on,* he thought.

All of a sudden, they heard a rumble. "What was that?" said Marigold.

The rumble got louder. The ground was shaking. "Uh-oh," said Austin. "AVALANCHE!"

Tons of blue snow tumbled down. The rumble was deafening. Thomas sprinted as fast as his exhausted legs could carry him.

As Thomas ran, he didn't see the small cliff that was approaching. He was supposed to go around it and go down, but Thomas was hardly looking where he was going. He tripped over the ledge and landed face first in snow and rocks.

Thomas didn't know what was worse, the pain or the cold that his face was smothered in. But he didn't have any time to choose. The avalanche was gaining on him fast.

Thomas hastily got up and kept running. He was exhausted, cold, and hurting badly. But he was probably in a better situation than his friends. His friends were probably buried already.

Thomas ran and ran. He really wanted to rest for a minute, or an hour, or a day. But he had to keep on running or be crushed by the avalanche.

The avalanche was too fast. It slammed into Thomas, and he tumbled down the mountain. He couldn't breathe. His mouth began to fill up with snow. He gagged and tried to pull the snow out of his mouth, but his arms were busy flailing about as he tumbled down the mountain.

Thomas didn't know when the avalanche stopped, but he knew that he was stuck in the snow, unable to move. He was lucky, though. He had an air pocket around him. The snow was melting in his mouth, too, thankfully, so he could breathe.

Thomas thought it had been about 20 minutes when he heard scratching above him. Two minutes later, Billy's head appeared. "It's Thomas!" he said.

Austin and Marigold ran over. "How did you get out?" Thomas asked.

"A furry tigo dug us out!" Billy explained.

Thomas climbed out. He was bruised, but he was lucky and hadn't hit any rocks. He just couldn't believe he was alive.

When Thomas climbed out, he saw a furtigo sniffing around and Mikey and Jane talking. "Nobody died?" Thomas asked, surprised.

"Austin and I dodged the avalanche, and a furtigo found Billy and dug him, Mikey and Jane out. The furtigo dug you out last. We thought you were dead. You were lucky enough to have an air pocket when the snow settled," Marigold explained.

Thomas noticed they were at the bottom of the mountain now. "At least we're down the mountain now," he said.

Mikey and Jane ran over. "We found a path," Mikey said. "Because we're way better at finding stuff than you. Were you even looking?"

Thomas ignored the snide remark. "Where's the path?" he asked.

"Just over there," Jane said, pointing. Thomas could see a sign with directions where she was pointing.

Everyone ran over. One of the paths went to the Land of Emerald Hail. They began down the trail.

The walk through the grassy savanna was long. They had been walking for over five hours, and Thomas saw no sign of the land of Emerald Hail.

Then Thomas saw a glint in the distance. Something was shining. The group crested a hill, and before Thomas was a forest. Except the ground was covered in shimmering green. "Whoa," Jane said. "This is beautiful."

The group walked down the hill. Thomas could see that the shining green stuff was tiny shards of... he didn't know. *Hail?* Thomas thought.

As the group got closer, the temperature dropped rapidly. *Strange,* Thomas thought.

When they got to the shining green stuff, Thomas picked a piece up. It felt like a rock-hard piece of ice, but it wasn't melting.

The group continued forward, and the farther in they went, the denser the green hail was, and the colder it got. A strong wind began howling through Thomas' ear. He looked at the darkening sky.

A massive green cloud was floating overhead. "Uhh guys," he warned. "I think we have a storm incoming."

"That storm looks weird," Austin said.

A piece of green hail bounced off Thomas' head. That's when he got it. The Land of Emerald Hail.

"Hailstorm!" he yelled. "Find shelter!"

The hail started coming down harder. It hurt more than normal hail did, or maybe it was just bigger.

Thomas sprinted down the path, searching for something to take shelter under. Then he noticed a small cavern partially covered by leaves. "Over here!" he called.

Everyone sprinted over as the hail continued to pound the ground harder and harder. Everyone piled inside the small cave.

Thomas shivered. This place was cold, and the storm was blocking the sun. "It's so cold," said Austin, as if reading Thomas' mind.

"Totally," Marigold agreed. "I hope this storm lets up soon."

The kids waited for hours, but the storm wasn't letting up. The sun was dropping now, and it was getting colder. "We need to huddle together to stay warm," Marigold said.

The kids huddled together as night washed over the land. Eventually, Thomas fell asleep.

Thomas was cold. Very cold. A blizzard was raging, and Thomas couldn't see a thing. A dark blue Barana swooped down behind Thomas. He tried to turn around and punch it or something, but he was frozen in place. The Barana called to more Baranas in its growling voice, and they grabbed Thomas, carrying him to the Barana fortress...

Thomas awoke to glass shattering. No, not glass. Hail. Huge pieces of hail three times the size of Thomas' head were coming down now. *Well, that will make it hard to sleep,* he thought.

Austin groaned and sat up. The hail must've woken him up too. Then a giant piece shattered just outside the cave, spraying Thomas with shards of emerald hail. "Ow!" he said as one cut into his arm.

That woke everyone else up. "It's still hailing," Marigold yawned.

"Apparently so," Austin grumbled.

"I wanna go home," Jane whined.

"If this hailstorm ever lets up, maybe," Thomas replied.

The hail grew and grew to the size of a large dog. The kids huddled in the back of the cave, trying to avoid shards of emerald hail.

Thomas heard a massive piece of hail shatter atop the cave. Then he heard the sound of cracking. He looked at everyone else, confused and nervous. They all looked the same.

And then the front of the cave collapsed down, closing the exit. The kids were trapped.

PART THREE

THE JEWEL OF ORDER

CHAPTER SIXTEEN

Thomas looked at the others, panicked. "We're trapped!" Austin cried. "We'll never escape this place!"

Everybody panicked. "We're doomed!" Jane agreed, pacing.

Thomas racked his brain for ideas. They could try to all push the rock together once the hail let up. They could hope some random elemental thing happened, moving the rock. He couldn't think of anything else.

Thomas' stomach growled. They didn't have any food or water. They needed to get out soon. "We need to sleep on this," Thomas said. "We need ideas for getting out."

Thomas expected Mikey to come back with a snide remark, but he didn't. He just grumbled, and they went to sleep again.

When Thomas woke up, Billy and Austin were already up, pushing on the rock. Mikey, Jane, and Marigold were also climbing to their feet.

"Let's all try pushing the rock together," Thomas said. "Maybe if we work together, we can move it."

Everyone walked over and pushed on the giant boulder. It didn't budge. "Harder!" Thomas urged. "Harder!"

It was fruitless. The kids worked on pushing the boulder for 30 minutes without any luck. Thomas' arms ached. He slumped down in the back of the cave, hopeless.

An hour later, Thomas was back up and at it, screaming through the small opening in the exit. "HELP!" he shouted. "HELP US PLEASE!" Nobody had even walked by yet.

Thomas screamed until his throat was dry, with no luck. Once again, he slumped down in the back of the cave.

Thomas' stomach growled again. He climbed back up and started shouting again.

Nobody ever walked by. It was like this place was deserted, and the kids would be stuck in this cave forever. Nobody would even find their bodies.

Everybody else yelled for some time too. They started taking shifts. But still, after an entire day, nobody ever came.

Thomas fell asleep that night, hopeless.

In the morning, they started up again, screaming for anybody who could help them. It was Thomas' turn. "PLEASE! SOMEBODY HELP US! PLEASE! HELP!"

Around noon, Thomas was screaming again. He didn't know how long he had been screaming, but he knew that his throat was so dry he couldn't make words. "PEAS! EP US!"

Then someone walked by. "HEP!" Thomas yelled; his hope restored.

The person turned. It was a man. A normal human. He had a curly mustache and short brown hair. "Oh! Hi!" he said. "Are you trapped?"

Thomas, unable to make words, just nodded. The others ran over. They waved, smiling.

Next thing Thomas knew, the man had cut a hole through the rock, and the kids were limping through. "Do you need anything?" the man asked.

"Wa-er," Thomas croaked.

The man pulled out some water bottles and filled them up with a blue jug. Once Thomas could talk, he said. "Thank you, who are you?"

"My name is Jeff," the man, Jeff, replied. "Who are you?"

The kids introduced themselves, and Jeff gave them some zorals. "So," Jeff asked. "Why are you guys out here in this dangerous place?"

"We're looking for a clue to find the Jewel of Order so we can stop the Barana monsters," Thomas explained.

"Oh, man!" Jeff said. "Those Baranas are evil! Would you be kind enough to let me help ya kids?"

"Of course!" Thomas agreed.

"Okay, so where are we headed?" Jeff asked.

"To the obsidian gulf," Thomas replied.

"Okay, then we'll have to follow this path and take the second left. That should get us there by the end of the day," said Jeff.

Everyone started down the path. "So," Thomas asked. "Is the obsidian gulf made out of obsidian?"

"Oh, no, no, no," Jeff said. "The water is just pitch black. Nobody knows why. I was actually on my way to study it myself!"

"Oh, cool!" Thomas said.

Thomas continued talking to Jeff for a while. Eventually, Jeff said, "Here's our turn!"

They turned onto the path. Thomas could barely see the obsidian gulf through the trees. The smell of saltwater drifted into his nose.

They walked down to the obsidian gulf. Jeff was right; the water was pitch black. *Weird,* Thomas thought.

"That looks like oil, not water!" said Jane.

"But it smells like saltwater, so it can't be oil!" said Austin.

"The clue should be somewhere around here," said Thomas.

Thomas pulled out the clue.

In a Land of Emerald Hail, the clue will prevail. Follow the sound of the howling wolf and find your next clue by the obsidian gulf.

"Maybe we have to follow the sound of the howling wolf!" he said.

"We should wait until night and listen for the wolf," Marigold added.

Night came fast. The group ate dinner, and the sun was down. "Okay, listen for a wolf," Austin said.

Everyone went silent. Thomas heard a howl. "I hear it," he whispered. "Follow me."

They walked across the sandy beach. The howl continued. It seemed to be coming from a little ways away.

They followed the howl into the forest. Thomas spotted something glowing in the night. "Maybe it's that!" he said.

Thomas walked over. A small button was hidden in a tree stump. Austin started to say something. "But the wolf sound isn't—"

Thomas pressed the button before Austin, hoping it might give him the clue. A high-pitched siren erupted from a hidden speaker, and the Baranas swarmed.

CHAPTER

SEVENTEEN

"Uh oh," said Jeff.

"I *told* you not to press it!" Austin said.

They all started to sprint away from the Barana attack.

"They're getting away!" growled a Barana.

"Well, duh," said another Barana. "C'mon, let's get 'em!"

The group struggled to run through the thick brush. Thomas almost tripped over a log.

Then they came out on the sand. The Baranas hadn't caught up yet, but they would soon. "Guys," said Thomas. "We can't just run. We need to fight!"

"Like in the taco place!" said Billy.

"The *fake* taco place," Mikey corrected.

Just then, they heard flapping wings. The Baranas were coming. "Get ready!" Thomas said.

The Baranas burst through the forest. Thomas leaped up and kicked a Barana in the face. "GLMPH!" the Barana said as Thomas' foot went into his mouth.

But seconds later, Thomas found himself surrounded by Baranas.

"Uh oh," he said.

The Baranas flew at him. But just before they grabbed him, Thomas felt a searing pain on his arm. *Am I on fire?* he thought.

He looked over. He wasn't on fire. His arm was glowing! The white glow was spreading all over him. He shook, trying to get it off, but it wouldn't. "What the heck?" Thomas said.

"Thomas!" Austin said. "You're glowing!"

"Thomas, you're glowing like a night light!" Marigold agreed.

The glow spread gradually to his legs as the Baranas picked him up. "Help!" Thomas screamed.

The Baranas split off and flew over the gulf. Thomas glowed brighter and brighter. Then, in shining light, the Baranas carrying Thomas disappeared.

Thomas fell into the Obsidian Gulf with a splash. The frigid water took him by surprise, but what really surprised him was how he had been glowing. Literally *glowing*, like a lamp.

The glowing thing stuck in his mind, puzzling him, as he swam through the jet-black water to shore. But he forgot about the fact that he had glowed when he saw the Baranas were gaining on his friends.

Thomas rejoined the fight, but he and everyone else were quickly overpowered. The Baranas swooped in, tentacles moving about, ready to wrap around the group and carry them into the sky.

Thomas heard a howl. He was just barely able to make out the silhouette of a huge wolf sprinting towards them. It seemed to be about six feet tall at the head. It was the biggest wolf Thomas had ever seen, though he'd only seen wolves in zoos.

It charged into the Baranas, biting some clean in half. Pretty soon, all the Baranas were dead or flying away.

"That was crazy," gasped Marigold.

"Yeah," agreed Austin. "And did you see Thomas glowing earlier?"

"Wait, Thomas the Train was glowing?" said Mikey. "Oh, well duh, he did! Do you think any of us missed the entire sky lighting up?"

"It was awesome!" said Billy. "Thomas made the turkeys explode in his face!"

"I wonder how that happened," said Jeff.

"Yeah," said Thomas. "It was weird. And that wolf!"

The wolf curled down. "Can I ride it?" Billy asked.

"No!" Austin said.

But Billy was already climbing on the wolf's back. "Billy! Get off!" Marigold ordered.

But the wolf was already up and carrying Billy away! "Billy!" Thomas said, running after the wolf. Everybody else followed.

They chased Billy and the wolf into the woods. They could hear Billy screaming with joy.

They chased Billy for about five minutes until the wolf stopped and let Billy off its back.

They were deep in the woods now. The combination of vines and trees blocked most of the moonlight, but little slivers still shone through.

The others soon caught up. "Don't do that," Marigold panted.

"The wolfie is so fun to ride on!" said Billy. "And he knows how to talk!"

"Hello," the wolf growled in a deep voice. "Your friend here sure loves riding me. Would you like me to lead you to the clue?"

"Of course!" Thomas agreed, surprised the wolf could, in fact, talk. But after everything that had happened, a talking wolf was only a little weird.

"All right," said the wolf. "Hop on my back."

Billy smiled and climbed on the wolf's back again. "Come on, kids! Get on Wolfie!" he said.

As they were climbing on, Mikey said, "You named him *Wolfie*?"

"Yeah!" Billy said. "He says that's his nickname! He's still a kid!"

"Wait... what?" Thomas said. "This wolf is almost six feet tall, and it's still a *kid*?"

"Yes, I am a kid," the wolf said. "And yes, my nickname is Wolfie. My real name is Coralon."

"I'll be calling you Coralon," Austin said. "Though Billy will probably call you Wolfie. Also, where did you learn to speak English?"

"You may think I am just a wolf based on instinct, but my species is just an evolved wolf. We're able to teach and learn other people's languages. We've learned to coexist with humans and other aliens." Coralon explained.

"Wow," Thomas said.

"Can you take us to the clue now?" Mikey asked.

Coralon got up and bounded off, Thomas clutching onto his soft fur. Billy was right. Riding on Coralon was fun.

After a few minutes, Thomas saw a rock that looked like a mini volcano. It started out flat and curved up to a 90-degree angle. When they got to it, Thomas saw that at the top, it sloped back down, forming a bowl shape. Inside was the clue.

"The clue!" said Thomas. He was surprised it was just there in plain sight. He got off Coralon and grabbed it.

Thomas looked at the clue in his hand. It read:

Congratulations! This is the last clue before you get the Jewel of Order. You are doing well, but you have to be careful. The Baranas are out there. It is never safe. Watch out! The clue is: Let the monkeys take you; the test will ensue. Dive down through the fire; this is very dire.

"Let the monkeys take you?" said Mikey. "We're gonna be taken by *monkeys*?!"

"Yay!" said Billy. "I love monkeys! Monkeys are my second favorite animal after bruhs!"

"Dive down through the fire," said Marigold. "That sounds scary."

"We need to stay somewhere safe for the night," said Austin.

"I was staying in a little cabin in the forest before I saved you kids," said Jeff. "We could stay there."

"Great!" said Austin. They started towards the forest, with Jeff leading them.

A little while later, Jeff announced that they were nearly at the cabin. Thomas had been enjoying the walk, with the moonlight washing over the whole forest.

Then Thomas heard someone crying. He looked around. Nobody was crying. *What's that crying sound?* Thomas thought.

They continued on the path. Then Thomas saw somebody crying on the side of the trail. The person looked about six or seven.

Thomas went up to get a closer look at the crying person. When he saw her face, he gasped.

"Dana?!"

CHAPTER EIGHTEEN

Dana looked up. Her face was wet with tears, and her eyes were red from crying. "Tom-Tom!" she said.

Usually, Thomas would snap at her to not call him Tom-Tom, but he didn't feel like snapping. His sister was sad, and he never snapped at Dana when she was sad.

"Dana!" said Thomas. "How did you get here?"

Dana drew a shuddery breath. "I went to the clashroom to see if it was really the clashroom. But then it was, and I got sucked away! Then there were these monsters, and they were trying to get me, and I ran away."

Dana stood up and hugged Thomas, sobbing. "This place is so scary. I want to go home!"

Thomas felt surprised because Dana had never actually hugged him before. He also felt angry. "You broke into the clashroom?"

"Yes! Please don't be mad at me. I want to go home!"

Typically, Thomas would've been furious at Dana, but this time he just couldn't yell at her. She was so scared.

"So, this is your little sister?" asked Jeff.

"Yeah, she's my little sister," answered Thomas.

"What's your name, kid?" said Jeff in a kind voice. Dana gazed up at Jeff and rubbed her eyes.

"Dana," she mumbled. Then, with surprise, she added. "Careful Tom-Tom! There's a giant wolf behind you!"

"He's our friend," Thomas said.

"Hello," Coralon said in a gentle voice.

"It TALKS?" Dana asked, surprised.

"It does," Thomas said. "Come on, Dana, we need to get to Jeff's cabin before I explain everything." Thomas pointed to Jeff.

"I just want to go home!" Dana cried. "Not to a cabin!"

"Don't worry, Dana," said Jeff. "We'll get you back home."

Dana drew another shuddery breath. "Really?"

"Yes. Come with us."

Dana let go of Thomas' shirt and held Jeff's hand. They continued walking.

"Geez, Thomas," said Mikey. "Your sister is just like you. Such a crybaby."

"She's not a crybaby," said Thomas. "She's just scared. She's barely seven, you know."

"Such a scaredy-cat," mumbled Mikey.

"Don't blame her. This universe is pretty scary compared to our home universe," said Thomas. "Plus, the Baranas were probably trying to attack her."

Pretty soon, they arrived at Jeff's cabin. It was similar to Freddy's house and pretty nice, too. Once they got inside, Jeff gave them a nice late-night snack of...tacos!

"Yummy! Tacos!" said Dana, stuffing an entire chicken taco in her mouth.

"Mmm! Are these tacos from Tony's Terrific Tacos?" said Austin.

"Yep!" said Jeff.

"Where?" asked Dana.

"Tony's Terrific Tacos," Thomas said. "It's a taco place in this universe. Their tacos are *delicious*."

After the delicious dinner of tacos, everyone settled down to sleep. The boys shared a room, the girls shared a room, and Jeff had his own room. This time, Thomas got to sleep easily. He was exhausted.

Thomas was walking all alone down a golden path. It looked like the yellow brick road from *The Wizard of Oz.*

Then the sky, which had been blue and cloudless before, turned jet black. The golden path turned a dull gray. Lots of Baranas appeared out of thin air.

Thomas tried to fight, but he couldn't move. The Baranas were attacking him nonstop.

Then he started glowing like it did by the Obsidian Gulf. All the Baranas disappeared. Then everybody he knew appeared and started congratulating him.

Thomas woke up. The room was pitch dark. All he knew was that everyone was asleep. Even Billy! The only thing he could hear was Austin's snoring from across the room.

Thomas rolled over and tried to go back to sleep, but he couldn't. His dream stuck in his head. What could it mean?

Then Thomas heard something splat against the window. He gasped. It was...Baranas! Lots of Baranas! They were trying to break in!

Thomas heard Austin, Mikey, and Billy wake up. Even though it was pitch dark in the room once again, Thomas could tell they were shocked when they saw the Baranas.

"The turkeys are here!" screamed Billy.

"They're Baranas," Thomas said.

"Turkeys!" Billy screeched.

At that moment, Jeff ran in. Jane, Dana, and Marigold were behind him. They all looked alarmed.

"Those Baranas are going to break in any second and burn this house down!" Jeff said, alarmed. "We have to defeat them before that happens, or we'll all be burned to a crisp!"

"No! They're scary!" Dana said.

"Well, we can't just let them break in," said Thomas.

Dana looked horrified as the rest of the group went outside to fight the Baranas. She stayed inside, watching the group from a window.

The Baranas were shocked to see the gang standing outside. "How did you get out here?" said the leader.

"Um...through the door," said Austin, pointing to the front door.

The leader of the Barana army looked at the front door in anger. Then he breathed fire at it. The front door burst into flames and burnt to ashes in seconds. Dana screamed inside the house.

"There. Now there isn't a front door," said the leader.

"That wasn't necessary," said Austin.

"Turkeys burned down the door! Noo!" screamed Billy.

The leader Barana growled and breathed fire straight at Thomas. Thomas dodged each fireball, leaped up, and punched the leader Barana in the face.

The leader howled in pain, but he wasn't defeated. Baranas came zooming at Thomas from every direction.

Thomas hoped for an elemental miracle but then remembered the fake taco place fight. *I have to fight for myself,* he thought.

Thomas jumped up, spun around, and kicked each Barana. They fell to the ground.

"How did one wimpy boy do that?" growled the leader.

As the leader said this, Austin was sneaking up on him. Then Austin punched the leader. The leader fell to the ground.

At first, Thomas thought they had defeated the leader, but then the leader sprung up and started shooting slime at the group.

Everyone managed to dodge the slime, but Marigold was unlucky.

"Ha!" said the leader. "We've got one!" Marigold tried desperately to escape the slime, but she couldn't. A bunch of Baranas zoomed towards her, ready to grab her.

Thomas wouldn't let that happen. He leaped to pull Marigold from the slime. Just as he did that, he felt tingly.

Thomas felt like everything was in slow motion. He was soaring through the air, and then his skin started to glow, just like in the Obsidian Gulf. This time it spread much quicker. Pretty soon, the light was huge.

Thomas leaped onto Marigold, pulled her out of the slime, and they both fell onto the ground. Colorful light surrounded the nearby Baranas, and the Baranas disappeared in thin air! "Whoa!" said Marigold. Thomas smiled.

"What?!" said the leader Barana. "Those troopers just vanished!"

"I know, right?" said another Barana. "But good thing I'm still here." Then he flew towards Thomas and Marigold. He tried to grab them, but he missed.

"You darn kids!" said the Barana. He tried again, missing Thomas by inches. Marigold snuck up on him and punched him, knocking him out.

Meanwhile, two Baranas were swooping towards Austin. He knocked them out with a punch.

Then a group of Baranas all attacked Marigold! "Why am I the favorite?" she asked. She kicked and punched, but the Baranas grabbed her!

Thomas leaped up, pulling five Baranas off Marigold, but the other 10 flew into the sky with Marigold. "Marigold!" screamed Thomas.

"Loverboy," said Mikey as he fought away a couple of Baranas. Jane giggled.

"Why are you laughing?" said Austin. "You're the serious couple!"

"We need to save Marigold!" said Thomas, ignoring Mikey's remark.

"How are we supposed to save her?" said Mikey. "She was taken into the sky!"

"If we try to save her now, we'll have no hope," said Jeff. "We need The Jewel of Order to defeat the Baranas."

They decided to make a plan to defeat the remaining Baranas. Then they put their plan in action.

"Hey!" said the leader. "The kids are distracted, so kill them! They might kill King Barana, and then we will be dead! So kill them!"

"But, Paaaaa!" said another Barana.

"I'm not yo papa!" shouted the leader.

"Hey!" said Mikey. "The Baranas are distracted, so kill them! They might kill the multiverse, and then we will be dead! So kill them!"

"But, Paaaa!" said Jane.

"I'm not yo papa!" said Mikey.

"Copycat," said the leader Barana.

"Copycat," said the other Barana.

"Copycat," said Mikey.

"Copycat," said Jane.

"YOU STUPID KIDS!" roared the leader. He breathed lots of fire.

"YOU STUPID BARANAS!" yelled Mikey. He burped a lot.

Thomas, Austin, Billy, and Jeff were now behind the Baranas. Thomas did a spinning leap to take out 15 Baranas while Austin, Billy, and Jeff took out 10. "Hey!" said the leader.

"WEEEEE!" yelled someone. Everyone turned around.

Thomas saw Dana running towards the group! She stopped by Thomas. "Tom-Tom!" she said, hugging Thomas.

"Dana, what are you doing?" said Thomas.

"I wanna help you," said Dana.

"But five minutes ago, you were super scared," said Thomas.

"That was five minutes ago," said Dana. "Now I'm gonna help you."

"Yay!" shouted Billy.

Dana turned towards the Baranas with determination. Then she rushed at them. She punched one in the face. "Hiya!" Dana said. "I do kung fu!"

"Good for you," cackled the Barana. "You're coming with us."

"No way!" yelled Dana. She kicked the same Barana. "I don't wanna go with you guys!"

"What happened?" murmured Austin. "She was crazy scared five minutes ago."

"I have no idea," Thomas said.

Dana was going crazy. She was flinging her fists around, punching every Barana near her. She was also kicking her legs, even though she was standing up. And if a Barana tried to attack her, she would bite it.

"Get that crazy girl!" yelled the leader.

"We're trying," said a Barana. "But she's a killing machine. She'll kill any Barana who gets near her."

"Well, try harder!" yelled the leader. "King Barana ordered us to get these children! Go!"

The Barana, who was scared of Dana by now, followed the leader's order. But he was knocked unconscious three seconds later.

But the battle wasn't over. Almost 200 Baranas remained. "You will be coming with me!" the leader Barana cackled. "Promotion, here I come!"

"What's a promotion?" Dana asked.

"Is this child stupid?" the leader Barana growled.

"No!" Dana said. "I'm Kung Fu Panda!"

"Who's that?" the Leader Barana.

"Me!" Dana said.

Then she leaped up, kicking a Barana in the eye and sending him tumbling into three Baranas behind him. "Your sister learning kung fu?" Jeff asked.

"Six days a week," Thomas replied with a smile.

As if on cue, Dana did a spinning kick, taking out multiple Baranas. "Well, we should help her!" Austin said.

They did. They attacked the Baranas fast, but they were delayed, and the Baranas outnumbered them. It would be almost impossible for them to defeat the Baranas without help from the mysterious elemental forces.

The Baranas were advancing on the kids. Even Dana was having trouble. "I shall finally end this dilemma!" the leader Barana said. "Now I will *certainly* become Commander Eyeflame!"

The Baranas reached out with their tentacles, prepared to capture the kids and carry them through the sky. Dana started crying. "The monsters are going to get us!" she cried.

Then a deep voice said, "Not if we fight."

CHAPTER NINETEEN

Thomas looked towards the sound, confused about who was talking. Then he saw Coralon and his entire pack rush in and attack the Baranas. The adult wolves were almost ten feet tall!

The Baranas were not prepared. They didn't know how to fight the wolves, and the wolves destroyed every single one in moments, even the leader!

"Wow! Thanks, Coralon!" Thomas said.

"Thanks, Wolfie!" Billy agreed.

"This is my pack," Coralon said. "They agreed to help fight your enemies. They do not want the Baranas to take over this land. We will help you in any way we can."

Everyone cheered.

"Can we have eggs now?" said Dana.

Thomas looked back at the cabin. It was in ruins. An hour ago, it was fine, but now it was nothing but a pile of ashes and a few wooden planks.

"We can't have eggs since the cabin is destroyed," said Jeff.

Dana stared at the ruins of the house. At first, her face was emotionless. Then she scrunched up her face and started to cry.

"Eggs," Dana mumbled. "I want eggs." She was crying surprisingly quietly because when she cried, she usually bawled loudly. But now, she was silently sobbing.

One of the smaller wolves, maybe five feet tall, padded up to Dana. "It's okay," they said. "We can have eggs. We have eggs and chicken coops back in our den complex.

Dana's face lit up. "Really?" she said.

"Really," the wolf confirmed.

Dana yawned. "You seem tired," another wolf said. "Would you like to ride on my back?"

Dana yawned again and climbed onto the wolf's back. They had barely started moving when she fell asleep.

Ten minutes later, they arrived. Dana opened her eyes. She beamed when she saw the den. "EGGS!" she yelled, running into the den.

Even though it was still early in the morning, the wolves made scrambled eggs for everyone. They were amazing. The wolves had made enough for everyone to have seconds, thirds, and even fourths.

After the eggs, Thomas went back to bed. He felt exhausted after the whole fight against the Baranas. He fell onto his bed and fell asleep instantly.

An hour later, Thomas woke up. He crawled out of bed and looked out the window. Outside was the most beautiful sunrise he had ever seen.

He walked outside, marveling at the sunrise. The sky was lighting up with striations of yellow, orange, red, and pink, all mixing in what seemed like it could only be a painting.

Thomas walked back inside the den. He saw a wolf making bagels. He saw Billy playing Bruh the Kid. This place was a lot like a human home.

"Can I play with you?" Thomas asked.

"Yeet Yes Yeah Yote Yay!" Billy replied.

Thomas sat down in a wooden chair and grabbed a controller. He turned it on and joined the game.

Billy was Bruh the Kid. Thomas was Bro the Lid. Thomas was a lid, but he could fly. Billy was a kid. They had to complete the quest of rescuing Bobby Joe from a villainous cardboard box.

Unfortunately, the villainous cardboard box, AKA Eb, had an army of boxes with armor and swords. Billy whacked a box's lid, and it flipped over, making a ping sound, and giving Billy one gold coin. Thomas thought it was the craziest, most random game ever, but it was still surprisingly fun.

Thomas and Billy completed that level quickly. Thomas only lost one heart. Then he heard Coralon padding in. "Breakfast is ready," he said.

Thomas walked to the dining room. It was huge. It had a giant table with wolves lining its edge, chairs were out for the humans. Thomas sat down by Austin.

There was a huge assortment of bagels. Green chile, poppy seed, plain, cinnamon, blueberry, and others, too many to count! They also had butter and cream cheese. It seemed just like food in their home universe. Thomas chose a green chile bagel with butter. It was the most delicious bagel he'd ever had.

"Those bagels were delicious!" Jeff said after the bagel fiesta.

"Thank you," said the wolf who had made the bagels.

"No, thank *you*!" said Jeff.

"Weirdly, bagels exist in this place, too," said Mikey.

"Yeah," said Jane. "But still, they were good."

After breakfast, the people climbed up onto the wolves, and they left on their journey. But when they got out, there was a big surprise waiting for them.

CHAPTER TWENTY

"Marigold," Thomas exclaimed.

"How did you escape?" Austin asked.

"It wasn't that hard," said Marigold. "I just slipped through the bars and snuck out. The Baranas aren't that smart when it comes to perception like that."

"Huh," Mikey said. "Well, they do only have one eye."

"But how did you get all the way over here? The new Barana fortress must be far from here," said Jane.

"A faropa helped me!" said Marigold, smiling. "Weird thing was, I heard a voice in my head sometimes when I was with him."

"Weird," Thomas said.

"We're glad you're back!" said Coralon. "We were worried that the Baranas had done something horrible to you."

"We had bagels!" said Billy. "The wolfies gave us bagels, and they were yummy!"

"Lucky!" said Marigold.

"Now that Marigold is here, we can continue on our quest for the Jewel of Order," said Jeff.

Oh yeah! Thomas thought. With all the other stuff that had been going on, he had almost forgotten about that.

Thomas took the clue from his pocket and straightened it the best he could. "Let the monkeys take you; the test will ensue. Dive down through the fire; this is very dire," he read aloud.

"That's still a really confusing clue," Mikey said. "Why are we being taken by monkeys? And why are we diving down through the fire?"

"It's the last clue before we find the Jewel of Order," said Jeff.

"But what are we supposed to do? Just hang around until monkeys come and take us?" said Jane.

"I dunno," Austin said.

They walked away from the den, across the small clearing it was in. "Where are we supposed to go?" said Marigold.

Jeff pointed to a nearby path. "We could follow that path."

"But that might lead us in the completely wrong direction!" Mikey exclaimed.

"It's worth a try," said Thomas.

Billy hurried onto the path. "C'mon!" he said. "I wanna see the monkeys!"

Everyone followed Billy onto the path. It led into deep vines. The vines blocked out most of the sunlight. Only little slivers snuck their way through the thick vines.

"I have a feeling we're not going the right way," murmured Thomas. He didn't think anyone heard him, though.

They kept walking through the vines. The path seemed to go on forever. Thomas felt like he was just on a hike. A hike on a tiny trail through thick purple vines.

About fifteen minutes later, the path started to slope down. Thomas had been in the middle of the group up until now. Now he wanted to be up front.

Thomas tried to silently sneak through and take the lead, but suddenly he heard something coming. Something coming through the vines above them.

Then a bunch of drones came into view! And these weren't the little drones Thomas sometimes saw at the park, controlled by someone with a remote control. These were huge. The biggest ones were the size of a small car! And there were so many of them.

Thomas had only a millisecond to react. He ran. Thomas darted into the vines, away from the strange drones. After a few seconds, he was deep in the vines, but he could still see the drones and his friends.

Thomas could see huge metal claws coming about from the drones and grabbing his friends. *Maybe they're Barana drones!* Thomas thought. But why did they have drones all of a sudden instead of just reaching with their tentacles like they usually did?

Thomas started to creep slowly out of the vines, prepared to fight these drones. He planned to come out of the vines and catch them by surprise.

But before he could, one of the drones noticed him. It started to come into the vines towards him!

Thomas tried to run, but the metal claw caught him. The drones hadn't captured the wolves, luckily. But the drones had started to fly up into the sky, too high for the wolves to reach.

As Thomas came out of the thick dome of vines and went high into the sky, he knew for sure that he was doomed.

Chapter Twenty-One

Thomas awoke. He was in a bed with silk sheets and the softest, bounciest mattress ever in a seemingly golden room. *Why did the Baranas put us in a luxurious room?* Thomas thought, confused.

The others were in nearby beds. *I wonder what Billy thinks of this,* Thomas thought.

As if on cue, Billy triple backflipped off his bed, sticking the landing! "Woohoo!" he said.

"Breakfast!" a voice called out.

A zoobaquel walked into the room, holding glasses of orange juice. Immediately, Thomas knew it was an advanced zoobaquel. Then he realized the drones belonged to the zoobaquels! They were the monkeys that they were taken by! This was where they would get the Jewel of Order!

The zoobaquel served the orange juice to Thomas and the others. Thomas slowly drank his glass. It was nice and cold.

Then a zoobaquel brought in a delicious triple berry smoothie. "Yum!" said Thomas, licking his lips.

"Thank you!" said Jeff as he happily drank his smoothie.

"Oh my gosh! I love smoothies!" said Jane.

Next, another zoobaquel carried a plate of bacon! Thomas devoured the bacon.

"I want eggs!" Dana shrieked. "Bacon and eggs!"

Two zoobaquels hurried the next dish in –breakfast burritos! With egg, potato, cheese, and bacon!

"Mmm!" said Austin, eating his breakfast burrito.

"Guys...we shouldn't overeat," said Thomas.

"No worries," said a zoobaquel. "We use the Super Calorie Shrinker 3,000, so everything we give you is only a total of 300 calories!"

Just then, another zoobaquel entered the room, carrying a platter of pancakes. "Yum!" said Thomas. He loved pancakes!

Everyone enjoyed the pancakes, which were soaked in maple syrup. Then for the next fifteen minutes, they enjoyed sausages, waffles, yogurt, and of course, eggs.

After breakfast, another zoobaquel came into the room.

"Hello there," he said. "My name is Larkin. I will help you defeat the Baranas."

"Thanks!" said Jeff. "We could really use some help. I was a police officer back in my home universe, but I've never dealt with an empire like the Baranas."

"You must complete the test," Larkin said. "To get the Awesome Prize."

"Well, what's the test?" Mikey asked.

"You must jump into the burning bananas," said Larkin.

"Cool!" said Austin.

"Bananas? Why bananas?" Thomas asked.

"Because they are very plentiful, and we don't want to burn the forest," Larkin replied.

"Ooh! Me! Me! I wanna jump on the bananas! Let me!" blurted Billy.

"Are you, Billy, uh, I don't know your last name, willing to make the sacrifice to retrieve the Awesome Prize?" Larkin asked.

"Duh!" said Billy.

"It shall be known that you, Billy, are brave enough to leap into the fire to retrieve the Awesome Prize," said Larkin.

"I'm sure the prize isn't *that* amazing," said Mikey. "Probably one of those cheap nick-nacks."

Larkin led them out of the room. Soon they got to a pit full of swirling goop.

"Burning banana pit," said Larkin. "Jump through, and then you can get the Awesome Prize!"

Billy immediately jumped into the pit. "WEEEEEEE!" he shouted, falling.

He splashed into the goop, and Thomas couldn't see him. Some goop splashed up near the ring of the pit, but it didn't touch anyone.

They waited for five minutes, but Billy didn't arrive. Thomas was worried. Was Billy dead?

Then Billy danced into the room! "Hooray! I want the Awesome Prize!" he yelled.

"Billy!" said Thomas.

"He was only gone for five minutes, Thomas the Train," said Mikey.

"5 minutes and three seconds!" said Marigold. "I timed it on my watch, Mikey the Menace!"

"Don't call me that! And who cares about three seconds?" said Mikey.

"We do!" said Dana.

A zoobaquel stepped into the room. "Here is your prize!" it said, giving them a blue-green bouncy ball.

"Told you it was a cheap nick-nack," Mikey sighed.

They started to bounce the ball. "WAIT!" Larkin said. "Wrong prize! That's the prize for the balloon dart game!"

"What balloon dart game?" said Austin.

"*The* balloon dart game. Here is your *actual* prize." Larkin gave them a large, blue-green gem.

"Is that?" asked Austin.

"Whoa," said Thomas. "It's The Jewel of Order!"

"That felt way too easy to get, though," Austin said.

"Well, it wasn't easy for Billy!" Thomas said. "He dove through a pit of burning bananas!"

"You have completed the test," Larkin said. "You are worthy of this prize."

"No," a growly voice came. "It's mine!"

Thomas turned. King Barana had found them.

CHAPTER TWENTY-TWO

"Uh oh…" said Austin.

"Give me the jewel," growled King Barana.

"No!" said Thomas hastily. He didn't know what he was doing, talking back to King Barana.

"Oh, you ridiculous kids," said King Barana. "I said, *give me the jewel.*"

Next thing Thomas knew, flames were flying at the entire group. Thomas managed to dodge everyone, but he wouldn't be that lucky for long, he didn't think.

Then he heard a yelp. Dana's hand had been scorched by a fireball! "Dana!" Thomas said.

King Barana laughed. "You see how hopeless you are? That jewel is mine!"

Thomas clutched the Jewel of Order even tighter in his hand. The jewel that would save the multiverse. "It's not yours!" he said.

Then Thomas caught sight of the bouncy ball lying on the ground. It was the same color as the jewel. He had a plan.

Thomas slid under a fireball and ran to the bouncy ball. "What are you doing, Thomas the Train?" said Mikey.

Thomas had to jump over and slide under several fireballs. Still, he managed to grab the bouncy ball without getting fried.

Thomas made sure King Barana couldn't see the real Jewel of Order, and then he held up the bouncy ball.

"Hey, King Barana!" shouted Thomas. "You want the jewel? Here!"

Thomas tossed the bouncy ball over to King Barana. It hit him in the head.

King Barana scooped up the bouncy ball like a child who had just gotten a new toy. "The jewel!" he said. The bouncy ball in his tentacle, he flew away.

"Lord Turkey is a dum-dum!" Billy said. "He just took a bouncy ball!"

Marigold sighed. "His name is King Barana."

"We have not won yet. Now we must prepare for the final battle against the Baranas," said Larkin. "Time to design some weapons!"

"Weapons? Final battle?" Thomas felt a wave of anxiety. Despite all he had been through, he didn't think he would be ready to fight a bunch of Baranas.

"Banana that kills!" Billy blurted.

"One killer banana," said Larkin. He took out a notepad and wrote it down.

"A sword launcher!" said Jeff.

"Two," Larkin said. "A sword launcher."

"I want a yeeter gun! That shoots yeeter bombs!" said Billy.

"Three. A yeeter bomb launcher, but what does it do?" Larkin asked.

"A bomb that makes mini bombs when it blows up!" Billy said.

"A yeeter bomb launcher?" said Mikey, scowling. "That sounds ridiculous. I think we should have a laser sword."

"Four. Laser sword," said Larkin. "And we're keeping the yeeter bomb launcher."

Mikey grumbled. "How is a yeeter thing gonna help us?" he said. Larkin ignored him.

"I don't have any ideas!" whined Dana.

"That's okay," said Larkin. "Not everyone has to put in ideas."

"Blue flame launcher!" said Marigold.

"Ooh, good idea," said Larkin, writing it in. "Five. Blue flame launcher."

"Mini bomb launcher!" said Austin.

"Unique ideas!" said Larkin, writing it in. "I am going to send these ideas to my assistant, Quellzooba. He and our scientists will have them developed in no time!"

"Okay," said Thomas.

Soon, Larkin came back holding a yellow, banana-shaped object. "The Killer Banana is ready," he said. "We can test it on our fake Baranas."

"Ooh la la!" yelled Billy. He grabbed the Killer Banana, and ran off with it.

"Hey!" yelled Larkin. "Come back with that!"

Luckily, Billy did as instructed. They walked to a room. "This is the testing room," said Larkin. "We will test the Killer Banana now."

Ten very realistic but fake Baranas came up. "We need a volunteer," said Larkin.

Billy, of course, volunteered. He entered the chamber. Larkin pressed a button on the banana and threw it into the room. A timer counted down. *Three...two...one...*

The banana grew huge and got sharp edges. It spun through the air like a throwing star. Before anyone knew what was happening, the fake Baranas were cut in half.

"Oh wow!" said Thomas. He braced himself for something terrible, but... Billy was spared.

"Hooray!" he yelled.

"Um, Larkin," Thomas said. "We had some wolf friends. Can we get them?"

"Of course! Of course!" Larkin said. "We can get them soon, do not worry."

A zoobaquel with big goggles came in. *That must be Quellzooba,* thought Thomas.

"We finished the sword launcher," Quellzooba said.

"That's great!" said Jeff.

"We tested the killer banana, so you can make copies," said Larkin, handing Quellzooba the killer Banana.

He handed them a crossbow. "Test it," he said.

"That's just a crossbow!" said Mikey.

"Oh, but it isn't," said Quellzooba. "Well, kind of. It's a crossbow that launches swords."

Thomas took the crossbow, aimed it at a fake Barana, and fired. A small sword launched out. It went straight into the fake Barana's wing, and the fake Barana went up in flames! "Whoa!" said Thomas.

"That's a strong sword!" said Dana.

After two hours had passed, every weapon was ready and tested. "So, what do we do now?" Thomas asked.

"Uh, Thomas," Larkin said. "Come with me. There's something I need to check."

Thomas followed Larkin to a large room filled with other zoobaquels. "Uh, what is this?" Thomas asked.

"Thomas," Larkin said. "I just have this feeling, okay. Trust me."

They walked over to a chair. "Sit here to scan," Larkin said.

I'm being scanned? Thomas thought, *why?*

Thomas sat down in the chair, unsure of what was going on. The chair had a weird machine over the top of it, which must have been the scanner.

"Scanning now," said an automated voice. A bright yellow light beamed out of the machine and onto Thomas.

The yellow beam slowly crossed over Thomas. *What are they scanning me for?* Thomas thought.

Thomas opened his mouth to speak, but Larkin put a finger over his lips. "Shhh," he said.

Thomas obeyed and didn't speak. But he was still confused. Why was he being scanned? What was it checking for?

The beam crossed over Thomas' eyes, and he quickly shut them. He barely resisted the urge to yell, "Ow!"

The beam finished crossing over Thomas, then disappeared. The voice announced its discovery. "Superpowers confirmed."

PART FOUR

THE FINAL

BATTLE

CHAPTER TWENTY-THREE

Thomas gaped. "Superpowers?" he asked.

The automated voice continued. "Superpowers include: increased vocal waves, creating and destroying glowing, fireball conjuring, and wildfire starting. Your element is fire."

For a second, Thomas didn't believe what he had heard. *What?* he thought. *That can't be possible. This has to be a dream or* something!

Then Thomas remembered all the things that had happened. When he screamed so loud, the classroom - *clashroom* – shook. When had glowed and his enemies had disappeared. When fireballs randomly appeared. That had all been evidence of his powers.

Thomas walked back with the list of instructions on how to use his powers. As he read it aloud, he thought, *Maybe the fire stuff is how all that fire stuff happened earlier! But what about the other elemental stuff?*

"That explains the glowy thing!" said Dana when Thomas told everyone his powers.

"And screaming so loud the *clashroom* shakes!" said Mikey.

"And when the fireball hit the faropa!" added Marigold.

"Conjure a fireball!" said Austin.

"Okay, let's see," said Thomas.

He brought his hands up, moved them around, and put on all the pressure he could. Then... *POOF!* A small fireball began swirling in his hands! "Wow!" he said.

He threw the fireball straight into a fake Barana's face! *BOOM!* The surrounding Baranas blew up.

Thomas just stood there, amazed. He still sort of could not accept the fact that he had superpowers. For all this time, he was just an ordinary kid.

Everyone was silent. Then Mikey said, "How come you get superpowers? You're just some dork! I should have superpowers!"

"Quiet, or I'll attack you with a fireball," said Thomas.

Mikey immediately shut up. He obviously didn't want to be fireballed.

"Were you actually gonna attack him?" whispered Marigold.

"Nah," Thomas whispered back.

"I can't believe you have powers, Tom-Tom!" said Dana, enveloping Thomas in a giant hug.

"Uhh, guys," Larking said. "You should probably all get tested. We have this prophe-"

"Me, me, me!" Billy interrupted. Larkin took him into the room Thomas had gotten scanned.

Billy returned in a few minutes with a big smile on his face. "I have the superpowers!" he said. "I am the air! I can do the stuff!"

Thomas' eyes grew wide. Billy had powers too?

"What are his powers?" Austin asked.

"Windstorm starting, flying, and super speed," Larkin said.

"Okay, I so need to get tested," Austin said.

So, Austin left. And he came back with a smile on his face. Thomas knew it before Austin had to say it. He had powers too!

Austin said his powers were teleportation, making lightning storms, and shooting lightning out of his hands. His element was electricity.

But that wasn't it. Thomas' gape grew even wider when they learned they *all* had powers!

Marigold ended up with earth. She could make cracks in the ground, she could move things with her mind, cause earthquakes, shapeshift, and talk to animals.

Mikey's element was water. He could make tsunamis, make floods, make it rain or hail, breathe underwater, and he could also heal people.

Jane was space elemented. She could teleport, breathe in space, create portals, turn invisible, and had super speed.

Jeff and Dana got tested as well but didn't have powers.

"Marigold," Larkin said. "I just want to warn you. Be careful when you shapeshift. You can be a squirrel for like a day, but if you transform into a dragon, you can only do that for 10 minutes."

"Wait," Marigold said. "I can turn into a DRAGON?!"

"Yeah," Larkin said. "But only once during the battle, probably."

"Still, that is epic!" Marigold said.

"Yay!" Billy said. "We have the powers of yeet!"

"No way," Jeff said. "This is incredible!"

"That must explain all the mysterious stuff that happened earlier!" said Thomas.

"No fair!" said Dana. "How come you get powers, and I don't?"

"Dunno," said Austin, shrugging.

"Jane and I have the best powers," said Mikey. "Your powers are all as dumb as you are."

"Yeah," said Jane. "Space powers totally rock."

"Hey!" said Marigold. "That wasn't cool."

"Guys," Larkin said. "We have a prophecy, where the six most powerful kids in the multiverse come to fight evil."

"That sounds like us," said Marigold. "Wait, *is* it us?"

"There is a 99.999 percent chance that you are the children in the prophecy," said Larkin.

"So...in other words..." said Jane.

"So you kids are technically the children in the prophecy," said Larkin.

For a few moments, Thomas just let himself absorb that information. That he and his classmates were the most powerful kids in the multiverse. They were supposedly so awesome that they were stated in a prophecy to stop evil.

Austin finally spoke. "But we're just ordinary kids! We've never stopped any sort of evil before! We didn't even know we had powers until now!"

"You are still the children the prophecy states," said Quellzooba.

"He's correct," said Larkin. "You're the most powerful kids in the multiverse. You're destined to stop the Baranas! You must try, even if you fail!"

"So..." mumbled Thomas. "We were pulled here by destiny?"

"Indeed."

"But..."

"No ifs, no buts, no coconuts!" said Quellzooba. "You must stop the Baranas!"

"Tis true!" Billy agreed.

"All of a sudden you agree with them?" Mikey asked incredulously.

"We must stop the evil turkeys!" said Billy.

"You mean the Baranas," said Thomas.

"No!" said Billy. "The turkeys!"

Even though Billy insisted that the Baranas were turkeys, Thomas knew that he had to stop their evil plan.

CHAPTER TWENTY-FOUR

"We must continue preparing for the battles against the Baranas," said Larkin.

"Yeah!" agreed Billy.

"We have begun to gather dangerous creatures willing to fight against destruction," said Quellzooba.

"Wait, dangerous creatures?" said Thomas. "Do you mean the really dangerous ones, like relros and furtigos?"

"And then we can kill turkeys with furry tigos! I wanna ride a furry tigo!" shouted Billy.

"Calm down, Billy," said Larkin. "We shall keep preparing for the battle."

"Are you almost done gathering dangerous animals?" asked Jeff.

"Almost," said Larkin. "We just need about 10 more faropas and a few relros."

"Dangerous animals?!" said Dana. Her face went pale. "But dangerous animals are dangerous! They might kill us all!"

"Your sister is a super scaredy cat," said Mikey.

"I've told you! She's only seven!" Thomas said.

"Don't worry, we will tame the animals," said Quellzooba. But Dana still looked terrified.

"Who would like to help us gather animals?" asked Larkin. Nobody raised their hands...except for Marigold.

"Marigold?" said Thomas. It confused him. Marigold never did anything like that.

"Yeah," said Marigold. "I normally wouldn't do something like that, but my new powers might help me."

"I wanna go too!" Billy shouted, jumping up and down and waving his arms.

"Okay, Marigold and Billy will come with me to gather animals," said Larkin.

"What will the rest of us do?" asked Austin.

"Choose your weapons," Quellzooba replied.

Billy flew out of the window. "Weeee!" he shouted.

Larkin and Marigold jumped too, but Marigold used her powers to levitate them right before they hit the ground. Then she stopped. "Oof!" she said, crashing to the ground with a thump.

So, they continued. Lucky for them, there was a relro just outside. *Hi there,* said a voice in Marigold's head, *I'm Mr. Killer.*

Marigold looked at the relro. It looked at her expectantly. Marigold supposed it was talking to her.

"He says he's Mr. Killer," said Marigold to Larkin and Billy. To Mr. Killer, she thought, *we're making an army to fight against the Baranas. Wanna help?*

I will totally help you! replied Mr. Killer. *Us relros totally hate the Baranas.*

"He says he'll be happy to help," said Marigold.

"Great!" said Larkin. "Mr. Killer, welcome to our army!"

Later, Marigold, Billy, and Larkin returned with all the animals

they needed. "You're back!" said Thomas.

"How did it go? *Did you survive?*" said Dana.

"Um, they're here, so of course they survived," said Mikey.

"We are ghosts!" teased Larkin.

"No, you're not!" said Dana. She went up to Marigold and poked her finger into her ribs.

"Ow! What was that for?" said Marigold.

"See? You're not ghosts!" said Dana.

"I wanna ride a furry tigo!" said Billy. He immediately ran up to one of the furtigo enclosures. The four furtigos inside did not like that. They growled.

Billy didn't stop. He jumped right over the fence, landing on a furtigo's back! The furtigo roared but eventually got used to it. Soon it was bounding all over the cage, with Billy on top of it.

"What the!" said Jeff. "You've better be careful! Furtigos are dangerous!"

"Yeehaw!" hollered Billy.

He tried to stand up and twirl an invisible lasso. But he went flying off. He landed atop of not one, not two, not three, but all four furtigos standing on top of each other!

"What the?!" Mikey shrieked.

"YAY!" screamed Billy.

He tried to balance on top of all the furtigos, but he fell. He flew across the enclosure and landed next to Thomas.

"Well, that was insanity!" said Thomas. He was glad it was all over, but at the same time, he had laughed his head off.

"I want a pet furry tigo!" decided Billy. The furtigos all roared in agreement.

"I wanna bring a furry tigo to my house and feed it tacos, and name it Burger Bob!" said Billy.

"I don't think that will work," said Jeff. "Furtigos are huge and not native to your universe. Everyone would freak out if you had a pet furtigo."

"Yeah, plus your parents would be pretty freaked out," said Thomas.

"But Mama got me ten doggies!" said Billy in protest. Thomas had been to Billy's house a few times, and he actually had ten dogs.

"Anyway...our army is finished being built, and now the only thing you guys must do is choose your weapons," said Quellzooba.

Billy's face lit up like lights on a Christmas tree. "Killer banana!" he said. "And yeeter bomb launcher!"

Austin chose first. He chose the sword launcher. Thomas chose that as well.

Mikey chose the laser sword. So did Jane. "It's one of the only good ones," she said.

Marigold chose the blue flamethrower. "It's a really cool one," she said.

"The laser sword is better," Jane scoffed.

Meanwhile, Billy was grabbing his weapons. Of course, he chose the killer banana and the yeeter bomb launcher. "Hey, how come he got two?" said Mikey.

"You can all have two," said Larkin.

"Awesome!" said Austin. He chose the blue flamethrower.

Pretty soon, everybody had chosen two weapons. Only Thomas was left. "What are you gonna choose?" said Austin.

"Hmmm...," said Thomas. He found it hard to decide. There were so many choices!

"I'm getting impatient," sighed Mikey. "Can we just kill those monsters before they enslave everyone and everything?!"

Finally, Thomas chose the bomb launcher.

"NO!" Billy hollered. "WHY NOT THE YEETER BOMB LAUNCHER?"

"It doesn't matter right now, Billy," said Larkin. "We need to hop on the SUPER-FAST-MONKEY-MOVING-MACHINE, or SFMMM for short, and attack the Barana fortress."

"Okay," said Thomas as they walked out of the room.

"Oh," said Larkin. "By the way, only the most powerful people in the multiverse can hold the Jewel of Order without disintegrating. That would be you kids and, unfortunately, King Barana."

Thomas groaned. Of course, it just *had* to be King Barana. Besides, he was still taking in that he was one of the most powerful beings in the multiverse. It was still so weird to think about the fact that he and his friends had superpowers. Just a few days ago, he was just an average sixth grader.

They rode down the super-fast elevators to the bottom and walked out of the zoobaquel home. Outside was something that looked like a mansion with a turbo engine.

As Thomas walked in, he realized it really was a mansion with a turbo engine! Everyone except Jane and

Marigold ran straight for the door that said Gaming Room.

And of course, they started playing video games.

Larkin and other zoobaquels loaded up the final animals, and they left to attack the Barana fortress.

After about 15 minutes, the SFMMM stopped. *Are we already here?*

Thomas looked out the window. It turns out it was just loading on Coralon and the other wolves.

A while later, Thomas said, "Shouldn't we be there by now?"

"We are literally there right now!" said Austin, who was looking out the window.

Thomas joined Austin at the window. Outside, looming overhead, was the terrifyingly massive Barana fortress.

CHAPTER TWENTY-FIVE

Thomas climbed out of SFMMM and stared at the Barana fortress. It was massive. It could probably fit a billion Baranas, based on their size. How were they supposed to beat them, especially if not all the Baranas had arrived?

They formed a formation for their attack. The kids and wolves were in front, followed by the faropas, furtigos, relros, and finally, the zoobaquels.

Billy hopped on a fierce-looking furtigo. "Three...two...one..." Thomas counted down. "Go!"

They charged forward, Billy riding his furtigo, Jane running with super speed, Thomas and Marigold riding wolves, and Austin teleported.

Marigold used telekinesis and pulled a huge chunk of the wall out to let the kids in. "Throw that through the fortress!" Thomas yelled to Marigold.

The wall flew away, crushing some unseen Baranas. But when the dust cleared, Thomas almost fell off Coralon.

Hundreds of millions of Baranas were in the fortress. Thomas knew it could hold more, but seeing that many Baranas... it was all the more terrifying.

Baranas swooped out of the fortress, attacking the army before it had even entered. They swarmed, maybe a thousand of them.

Thomas was overwhelmed. As he ran, he conjured a fireball. He let it grow bigger and bigger and then threw it at the swarming Baranas.

It was too late. Almost all the Baranas were destroyed, but not before a furtigo roared in agony, swiping one last time, before falling. More Baranas were incoming.

"There's too many!" Austin said. "What do we do?"

Thomas had no reply. He started shooting bombs at the Baranas swarming above. Thomas was riding Coralon, who leaped up and swiped his tail.

Two beams of light shot out of Coralon's eyes, disintegrating hundreds of Baranas. Thomas saw another wolf doing it too.

"Did you do that?" Thomas asked.

"Yes, I did," Coralon replied.

"You have powers too?" Thomas asked.

"No, my entire species has a connection to the core of this planet. We're able to use it to our advantage. We don't know where it came from, but it sure is useful."

Thomas gaped. Coralon's entire species had laser eyes? It was crazy, yet also handy.

Thomas saw a furtigo swiping desperately at the Baranas around him. He shot a bomb into the middle of them, blowing some up.

Thomas shot another bomb but missed terribly. The Baranas were swarming too fast.

Then Thomas saw the zoobaquel drones swoop in, cutting the Baranas to pieces with their skillful aim.

Then Thomas saw the Baranas mounting up some kind of cannon. "Coralon," he said. "We need to take out that cannon!"

Coralon swerved and charged at the cannon. Thomas looked behind him and saw Marigold and Billy were following his lead. "Use your laser eyes!" Thomas told Coralon. "That will do some damage!"

Once again, two bright beams of light appeared. But the cannon had strong armor. Coralon wasn't able to get more than an inch through, even with Marigold's wolf also using laser eyes.

"What do we do?" Marigold asked.

Thomas didn't know. But as they got closer, he came up with an idea. "Let's take it over!" he replied.

Coralon charged forward. Thomas shot a bomb, taking out some of the Baranas. But almost 100 remained. Thomas marveled at the fact that just a few days ago, taking on 10 Baranas seemed impossible.

Thomas aimed and fired a sword straight into a Barana's face. The friction caught it on fire, and some of the Baranas around it caught on fire too. They tried to fly away but only succeeded in flying into some other Baranas. Thomas almost laughed.

The Baranas finished setting the cannon up. Thomas watched as it shot a drone down. *Poor zoobaquel,* he thought.

But then he saw the zoobaquel falling from the sky! It shot lasers with some kind of gun as it fell, then hit the ground with a thump and started shooting again.

Thomas looked back just in time to dodge a slime shot from a Barana on the cannon and shoot a sword into its wing. The Barana burned.

Billy charged ahead. "BURGER BOB GO!" he yelled.

His furtigo roared and ran faster. The Baranas' eyes went wide, and then Billy's furtigo, Burger Bob, smashed the Baranas on the cannon. They had overtaken it.

Thomas dismounted and stared at the controls. Everything lit up. But one button said: Shoot.

Thomas pressed it. A laser shot out of it, thankfully missing any zoobaquel drones.

Thomas saw what looked like a steering control and a screen showing where the cannon would shoot. He turned until he found another Barana cannon and fired. The cannon blew up in a cloud of smoke.

Thomas saw Jeff riding upon a wolf. "Jeff," he said. "Can you use this cannon?"

"Sure thing," Jeff asked. "How do I do it?"

Thomas showed him all the controls he knew. "Sounds good to me," Jeff said.

Thomas hopped back on Coralon, and he bounded off.

Thomas shot a fireball into a group of Baranas. They struggled to stay aloft and eventually fell to the ground, starting a small fire.

Thomas felt something bonk on his head. He looked up. Hail was falling from the sky, even though it was sunny. The hail grew bigger. Thomas saw the hail was hitting Baranas and knocking them out. *Geez,* Thomas thought, *these Baranas are weak!*

The Baranas fell to the ground, stunned by the hail. A group of furtigos led by Billy charged around, stomping on the unconscious Baranas.

Thomas heard something go off. He turned and saw Jeff firing lasers. His aim was terrific.

Then Thomas heard a rumbling. He turned and saw hundreds, maybe thousands, of small craft piloted by Baranas. They flew through the air, firing on the zoobaquel drones.

Thomas charged a group of Baranas. Coralon used his laser eyes, cutting them to bits. Thomas finished them off with a bomb.

Thomas heard the cannon again and saw a Barana ship crash down in a massive explosion. *BOOM!* It rattled the ground.

Thomas joined Austin in fighting a group of Baranas defending the entrance into the fortress. "We need to get in!" Austin said. "We need to defeat some Baranas before they can get into the fields. They're easier to kill when they're packed into a group!"

Thomas climbed off Coralon, who was lasering Baranas at the entrance, and threw a fireball into the swarming Baranas. "There's too many!" said Austin. "We need to get Billy or Marigold or someone!"

"Just hold them off for a few more minutes," Thomas said. "Coralon and I will go get Billy."

Thomas hopped on Coralon, and they took off. "Run faster, Coralon!" Thomas urged. Coralon sped up. Thomas got to Billy. "Billy," he said. "Come with me."

"Roger-roger!" Billy said.

Coralon turned around and sprinted back towards Austin. Billy and Burger Bob followed behind. Thomas saw that Austin was being pushed back. He brought down a lightning bolt, which forked across Baranas, killing them, but they were still swarming him.

Thomas launched a fireball. It punched a hole through the swarming Baranas, protecting Austin for now. But they needed to hurry.

Billy created a huge wind, pushing the Baranas back just enough for Billy and Thomas to get there. "Took you long enough!" Austin said.

"Coralon ran as fast as he could!" Thomas protested.

"Yeeter bomb go!" Billy yelled.

Billy shot a yeeter bomb into the Baranas. It blew up, taking out some Baranas. Then five mini explosions around it went off. "That is a cool weapon!" Austin said, using his blue flamethrower.

A Barana fired slime at Thomas. He dodged it just in time, but the Barana shot again, gluing Thomas to the spot. He began to feel weak. His legs crumpled beneath him. Everything was blurry. He heard Austin shouting, but it sounded muffled.

Thomas saw Austin get hit with the slime. Then Billy. They were stuck and weakening.

The Baranas cackled gleefully, reaching out with their tentacles. Thomas groaned. A tentacle wrapped around him, and he was carried into the fortress.

CHAPTER TWENTY-SIX

*B**OOM!*** A cannon shot blasted into the Baranas,
disintegrating them and the slime on Thomas, Austin, and
Billy.

Thomas fell to the ground with an "Oof!"

Jeff cheered far away. "Austin," Thomas said. "Looks like
the way has been cleared for you!"

Thomas pulled out the walkie-talkie Larkin had
given to him. He radioed to the zoobaquel. "I need a bag of
weapons," he said. "Repeat. I need 94 weapons."

Larkin's voice came through staticky. "On it, Thomas."

A minute later, a zoobaquel drone swooped in, dropping
the bag of weapons. Thomas grabbed it and ran into the fortress.

Fighting was going to be hard while carrying a bag of 94
weapons, so Thomas just dodged. But that was going to be hard, too.
There were a *lot* of Baranas in here, and they weren't happy.

Thomas dodged a slime attack and dove to the ground, narrowly avoiding another Barana's fire breath. He leaped and dodged, somehow avoiding every attack.

Then he noticed a grate up ahead. He dove away from another slime attack. He opened the grate, climbed in, and closed it just in time to dodge a stream of flame.

He crawled through the narrow passageway, dragging the bag behind him. He could hear Baranas struggling to open the grate with their tentacles now. He crawled faster.

Eventually, he found another grate and climbed out, just as the Baranas opened the other.

He came out in the long hallway of cages. Thomas glowed, and the locks on the cells sprung free. "Come on guys!" he yelled. "Grab a weapon and fight these monsters!"

A boy who looked about thirteen, with blond hair and green eyes ran over. He looked vaguely familiar. "Thank you so much," he said. "Who are you?"

"My name is Thomas."

"Thomas? Like Thomas Harlow?"

"Uh, yeah. What's your name?"

"Geon."

"Like, Geon Green?"

"Yes."

"Geon?"

"How do you know my last name?"

"GEON?!"

"Wait...THOMAS?!"

Thomas enveloped his old friend in a huge hug. "I thought you moved away!" he said. "You got sucked in the clashroom too?"

"Well, duh," his friend said with that goofy grin.

"Take a weapon, Geon; we have to fight these monsters."

Geon grabbed a blue flamethrower and started attacking Baranas. Thomas couldn't believe that his second-best friend was here. What other friends of his were here?

Thomas saw another boy come up. He had dark skin and a dome of curly black hair surrounding his head. "Who are you?" he asked.

"I'm Thomas," Thomas replied. "Who are you?"

"My name is Kaleb," the boy, Kaleb, said.

"Grab a weapon and start fighting," Thomas said.

Kaleb grabbed a laser sword, activated it, and ran at the Baranas. He cut them apart quickly and skillfully. It seemed like Kaleb had probably taken fencing lessons.

Kids rushed over to the bag of weapons, grabbing one and fighting off Baranas. Most of the kids were good, but were 100 kids a match for a hundred million Baranas?

"Work together!" Thomas yelled. "We need to get back to the open plains outside of here! Follow my lead!"

But before Thomas could yell something to the effect of "CHARGE!" a kid started blasting the walls with bombs.

Somehow, the wall gave way, and the kids charged into the field. Some of them were screaming battle cries. Some of them were purely focused on destroying Baranas.

Thomas led the charge. The kids ran through the field, destroying Baranas fast. More Baranas poured out of the holes in the fortress, cackling with laughter.

About 50 kids hung back, attacking the swarming Baranas. Thomas looked at the kids next to him. Geon and Kaleb. "Guys, help the others!" Thomas yelled. "Geon and Kaleb, you're with me!"

Thomas, Geon, and Kaleb split off, running towards Marigold, Austin, and Billy, along with Billy's group of furtigos and Coralon.

"Hi," Thomas said, hopping on Coralon.

"Hi," Coralon said. "Who are these?"

"Talking wolves?" Kaleb asked, jumping back.

"Don't worry," Thomas said, and then to Coralon, "I rescued the captive kids."

Baranas were everywhere, swarming. "I'm going after King Barana," Thomas said. "I need you guys to help me fight our way to the throne room."

"Let us help you!" Geon said. "We can fight King Barana together!"

"No," Thomas said, beginning to run for the fortress. "You guys need to help out here!"

"Please!" Geon pleaded. "Just let one of us!"

Thomas kept running. "Are you going to help me get there?" he asked.

Everyone ran up to his side. Geon made one last plea, "Please, Thomas. Please."

"Thomas," Austin said. "You can't defeat King Barana by yourself."

"Please," Marigold added. "Austin and Geon are right. You can't do this alone."

"Fine," Thomas said. "Geon, you can help me."

"Thank you," Geon breathed.

Then they were at the fortress wall, attacking. Thomas led the attack with a fireball. Geon and Kaleb gaped. "Do you..." Kaleb started.

"Yes, I do have superpowers," Thomas said. "And so do my friends here."

Geon and Kaleb's gapes got so wide Thomas thought they didn't even have jaws for a second.

Then a slime attack narrowly missed Thomas, bringing him back into the moment. He returned the favor by destroying the Barana with a sword from his sword launcher.

Thomas grabbed a Barana by the tentacle and swung it around, knocking out other Baranas. An outdated technique compared to his new weapons and superpowers, but still a useful one.

Thomas turned to Austin, panting a little. "Do you know where Mikey and Jane are?"

"I think they're still in the field. Why?" asked Austin.

"They might be in trouble or something," replied Thomas.

"Yeah, but just focus on killing Baranas!" Austin shrieked as a fire breath nearly hit him. He managed to dodge it by an inch.

The Baranas were everywhere. No matter how many Thomas took out, there seemed to always be more, shooting slime, breathing fire, grabbing at the kids with their tentacles.

Thomas threw a fireball into the Baranas, exploding some and burning others. Thomas launched three bombs back-to-back into the Baranas, blowing up almost 100.

The Baranas started to retreat a little bit, allowing Thomas a way into the fortress. Before he went in, he got an idea.

"Marigold?" he asked. "Do you think you can bring this entire wall down?"

"Cover me!" Marigold replied.

Thomas moved in front of Marigold, blocking any attacks from hitting her. Thomas started to feel the ground rumble. It was working! Then, the entire wall crashed down, smashing more Baranas than Thomas thought possible.

Jane appeared next to Austin. "Where did you come from?" Austin asked.

"Super speed!" Jane said, using a portal to suck a bunch of Baranas into space.

The Baranas were swarming over the wall now.

"Where is Mikey?" Austin asked.

"Flying a drone," Jane said.

As if on cue, a zoobaquel drone swooped in, firing on the swarming Baranas.

Thomas could see Mikey cheering in the cockpit. Then Thomas got an idea.

He created a massive wildfire across the downed wall. The Baranas, cackling with laughter, didn't even pay attention. They swooped through the fire, and when Thomas next saw them, they were gurgling on the ground.

Eventually, the fire let up because it had nothing but Baranas to burn, and the Baranas began to swarm again.

A laser blast scorched the air next to Thomas. He looked back and saw Jeff firing on the swarming Baranas.

"See ya guys later!" said Jane, and then she sped away.

Thomas could see a tiny bit of the door to the throne room. They only had to take out a couple hundred more Baranas, and then they would be at the throne room.

Thomas saw Kaleb move to the front, cutting Baranas to bits. He skillfully dodged every attack and then cut the attacker in half. Geon killed Baranas with blue flame, burning every Barana in his flamethrower's path.

Then, out of the blue, the Baranas began to push back.

"Woohoo!" Mikey said as he dove and dodged lasers.

He pulled up and fired a laser into a Barana ship's engine. Its flaming wreckage tore through the sky, landing in the fields.

Mikey dodged a laser from a Barana ship by inches, returning fire. Before he could hit it, a laser from Jeff's cannon cut it to pieces.

Mikey loved flying this drone. He could swerve and dive and pull up and fire lasers. *I am so taking this thing home!* he thought.

A laser came so close to hitting him that his ship charred a little bit, bringing him back from his reverie. *Focus Mikey, focus,* he thought.

He pulled up and fired on a Barana ship, breaking the cockpit glass and cutting through the entire ship. Lucky for him, the Baranas didn't have great aim.

A light on his board started blinking. He had a Barana on his tail, and they had a target lock!

"I've got one on my tail!" he yelled into his walkie talkie.

"I've gotcha covered," Larkin's voice replied.

The target lock light began blinking faster. They were getting ready to fire. Mikey braced for the shot to his engine, blowing him to bits before he could ever escape this terrible place.

Maybe Thomas is right, he thought, *perhaps I am a jerk. I thought I could fly this thing, and now I'm gonna die!*

Larkin's drone swooped in, destroying the Barana on his tail before it could fire. "Woohoo!" Mikey cheered.

He swerved right and fired his cannons, breaking a Barana ship to bits. He went into a barrel roll, narrowly avoiding another Barana target lock. Then he cut his engines.

He fell for a moment, and then the Barana pulled past. He reactivated the engines and swooped up behind the Barana. He waited for a target lock, almost...He fired! The shot took out the Barana's right wing, sending it rolling left. He fired again, taking out the right

227

engine! The ship was falling and taking a hard left. It crashed through the fortress, destroying a part of the roof.

The flaming wreckage destroyed Baranas Mikey couldn't see. "I think that your...classmates could use some help," Larkin's voice came again.

"I'll save 'em," Mikey replied.

Mikey swooped down to the fortress, away from the sky battle.

When he saw what was happening, his blood went cold. His...friends...were surrounded, and the Baranas were about to kill them!

CHAPTER TWENTY-SEVEN

Thomas saw a Barana get ready to breathe fire at him. He had nowhere to run. Then Mikey swooped in out of nowhere, peppering the Baranas with lasers.

Thomas' walkie talkie crackled. He picked it up. "You're welcome, my *friends*!" Mikey said.

"Did you just call *me* your friend?" Thomas asked,

"I sure did, *Thomas*!"

Well, that's nice, Thomas thought, *he didn't call me Thomas the Train!*

Pretty quickly, Mikey had shot down all the Baranas surrounding Thomas and his friends. The way to the throne room was clear.

Mikey flew away, and Thomas and Geon headed for the throne room. Thomas opened the massive doors, locking them behind him to keep any of his friends or any Baranas from coming in.

Thomas turned forward. In front of him, cackling with laughter, was King Barana.

Austin, Marigold, Billy, Kaleb, and Coralon bounded out of the fortress. "JANE! GET THAT PORTAL READY!" Austin yelled.

Almost a million Baranas were chasing them out of the fortress. They dashed out of the fortress, and right behind them, Jane's portal appeared. The Baranas had no time and flew right into it.

"Thanks for saving our hides," Kaleb said.

"In my case, literally," Coralon added.

"No problem," Jane replied. "Where are Thomas and his friend?"

"Hopefully not dead yet," Austin said.

Jane looked confused.

"Fighting King Barana," Marigold explained.

"Lord Turkey!" Billy said.

Billy turned around and threw his killer banana into a Barana. More were coming. "We gotta fight the turkeys!" Billy said.

"Baranas!" Marigold corrected.

"Turkeys!" Billy insisted.

Marigold sighed and gave up, levitating a tree and throwing it into the swarm of Baranas. Coralon's lasers cut a line through the Barana swarm, splitting them.

Austin brought down lightning bolts in each half of the swarm. The lightning jumped from Barana to Barana, killing or stunning all of them.

The first wave of Baranas was down, but more were incoming. The battle had just begun.

Mikey dove down, dodging a laser from a Barana ship and reversing the engines. The Barana ship sped in front of him. He pulled up to its level and fired before he even had a target lock.

The lasers peppered their engines, and it crashed down to the ground. Larkin's voice crackled through the walkie-talkie. "I've got two on my tail!"

Mikey swerved, chasing the Barana ships following Larkin. He fired, taking out the lead one. Larkin stopped, swerved, and fired on the other before the Baranas inside even knew what was happening.

Mikey looked at his screen. Only five drones remained, whereas more Barana fighters were leaving the fortress now. "We need reinforcements!" Mikey yelled into his walkie talkie. "We're down to five ships!"

Mikey heard someone say they had a Barana locking them. Then he heard screaming. He saw a zoobaquel drone dive down into the field, exploding on contact. "Make that four," he said with a sinking feeling.

Thomas' blood went cold. King Barana was the biggest Barana he had ever seen. This was different than when he'd seen King Barana at the zoobaquel fortress or when Freddy learned the Baranas had been the ones to invade his home universe. Those must've been decoys.

This King Barana was different. He looked like the Barana that was on the walls of the old Barana fortress. He actually had a serpent for a tentacle. Its eyes looked at him hungrily. Thomas flinched. Was King Barana actually two beings as one?

King Barana cackled. "Hello," he growled.

"Hi," Thomas stammered, struggling to hide his fear.

"You have come to kill me," he said.

"Of course I have," Thomas said.

Thomas shot a fireball at King Barana. King Barana easily flew away. Thomas shot two more fireballs.

Then King Barana did something that he'd seen no other Barana do. The serpent tentacle shot bolts of lightning out of its forked tongue! Thomas fell to the ground, barely ducking the attack. This Barana was more powerful than every other Barana combined.

Mikey dove down, narrowly avoiding Barana attacks. The Barana lasers, somehow, destroyed all the other zoobaquel ships. Only Mikey and Larkin remained.

Hundreds more Barana ships launched off the fortress roof. In seconds, Mikey and Larkin would be dead.

Then Mikey heard a rumbling. He looked at his screen. More white blips appeared. *More Baranas?* he thought.

The blips changed to green. Zoobaquel reinforcements had arrived!

Austin leaped, narrowly avoiding a slime attack. The second wave of Baranas had passed, and they were now fighting the biggest one yet. Almost 10,000 Baranas were swarming them. Austin brought down lightning bolt after lightning bolt. He was getting fatigued.

He turned around. The other kids weren't doing so well either.

Then he heard a scream. A Barana was carrying Dana away! Alarmed, Austin quickly shot a lightning bolt at the Barana. The Barana fell, surprisingly defeated by a small lightning bolt.

But now Dana was falling. She screamed as she tumbled towards the ground.

Austin ran to catch Dana. But he was too slow, too tired. Dana fell to the ground with a thump.

Austin ran up to Dana, though there was really nothing he could do.

Dana let out a moan. She was alive! But she was too weak to fight.

"Dana can't fight!" shouted Austin. "Bring in a drone!"

A drone swooped in, and a zoobaquel walked out. It picked up Dana and loaded her into the drone to take her to a medical station at the zoobaquel fortress.

Austin watched the drone fly away and ran back to rejoin the battle.

Austin shot blue flame into the swarming Baranas. They cackled with laughter, swooping forward.

He took a step back. The Baranas were overpowering them. He looked around, looking for a direction to retreat. There was only one direction the Baranas weren't. Back.

Austin got ready to teleport everyone away. Wait! That was it! Teleportation!

He ran forward, gaining momentum. "Hey, what is that kid doing?" a Barana asked.

"Austin! Stop!" Marigold yelled.

He activated his blue flamethrower. Then he leaped. He teleported above the Barana swarm. As soon as he had passed over the swarm, he teleported onto the ground.

The Baranas, surprised, panicked, looking around for Austin. While they were panicking, Jane created a portal. Almost half the Baranas flew in, thinking it was some sign of Austin. The portal closed, and only about one thousand Baranas remained.

Austin electrocuted the rest, and they fell to the ground, still sparking.

As soon as all the Baranas were on the ground, Austin saw it. A swarm of almost 20,000 Baranas was headed their way.

Thomas' vision blurred. He could barely make out the outline of King Barana, cackling with laughter. He said something, but it was muffled in Thomas' ear.

Thomas groaned and struggled to his feet. It took a heroic effort, but he reached out and slowly rose to his feet, barely balancing. He and Geon were going to need some luck if they were going to defeat King Barana.

King Barana launched another full-scale lighting attack at Thomas. The lightning hit Thomas this time. He fell to the ground, groaning in agony. "You puny little child!" King Barana cackled.

Thomas felt around, looking for a weapon. His fingers touched the sword launcher. He grabbed it and fired everywhere he could.

He heard King Barana roar. Thomas struggled to his feet. "I'm not puny," he said.

King Barana struggled to his feet. Thomas saw a sword had punctured his wing. "I may have a hurt wing, but I have lightning too," he growled.

Thomas saw Geon grabbing for his weapon. Geon picked up the blue flamethrower and turned it on.

The Baranas gained on them fast. Austin didn't know what to do. There was no way they would defeat all these Baranas!

Then Austin saw a laser pierce the air in front of him. Jeff was firing the cannons on the Barana swarm!

Austin breathed a sigh of relief. There were so many Baranas here, he didn't know how he was still alive.

More lasers peppered the Barana swarm. As the Barana swarm dissipated, Austin saw that no more waves were coming.

But he did see one thing. All the kids Thomas had freed. The Baranas were overpowering them, and fast.

King Barana began an attack of slime. Thomas struggled to dodge every attack. He saw Geon doing the same.

Thomas dove to the ground, dodging slime, and then leaped back to his feet, dodging another attack in the nick of time.

Thomas jumped up and grabbed a broken piece of the wall. He saw some slime stick just below him. He leaped off, avoiding the next attack, and tucking into a roll.

"I see that this is not working," King Barana growled.

King Barana fired lightning. But this time, it wasn't at Thomas, but at himself. The lightning crashed together, creating an orb. Then King Barana threw the orb at Thomas.

Thomas braced to die. He braced himself to have an electric orb destroy him.

The orb sped toward him. There was no dodging it. Then, out of nowhere, Geon dove in front of Thomas.

The orb sizzled and cracked, then dissipated. "Geon!" Thomas cried.

"Kill him," Geon rasped. "Kill King Barana."

Geon's head fell.

"Geon! No!"

CHAPTER TWENTY-EIGHT

Mikey cheered. Drones zoomed past, firing on the Baranas lifting off the fortress. Mikey joined them, smiling like he'd just gotten a new video game.

Mikey swooped down towards the fortress. He fired on the Barana ships struggling to take off while a hundred zoobaquel drones fired on them.

Soon, all the Barana ships would be gone, which would mean that the drones could help the people fighting on the ground.

Only a few ships remained. Mikey fired on them. Then he realized a light on his drone was blinking.

He needed fuel. He turned around and headed back towards the zoobaquel fortress.

Thomas roared with rage. He had an idea. He didn't know if it would work, but he was too angry to care.

He leaped up, grabbing a rope hanging from the ceiling. He had no idea why Baranas needed it, but he decided to turn it against them. He began to climb the rope. Once he was at a good height, he unleashed a massive spray of lava.

Now that his anger was dying down, Thomas was confused. The Power Checker Thingy didn't say he could make lava.

Thomas didn't know. Probably nobody knew why. But right now, Thomas was focused on climbing the rope.

The heat was fierce. He watched as a hunk of ceiling came down right next to him! Then he got an idea.

He swung the rope and grabbed the open ceiling. He heaved himself up and into the wonderfully cool air. He watched as a scorched King Barana fluttered up.

"I'm not finished yet!" he growled.

Thomas looked down. The lava was starting to melt the walls. The ceiling would fall in a matter of minutes.

Thomas faced King Barana and launched himself at him. They crashed to the ground, rolling and struggling.

Thomas took a tentacle to the face. He returned the favor by kicking King Barana in the eye. King Barana howled in pain and rage. He fired lightning into Thomas.

Thomas was thrown across the roof of the fortress. He didn't know how long he was flying through the air, but he knew that he flew off the edge.

Austin teleported to where the captured kids were fighting and began to help. He saw his friends follow.

The kids were retreating when Marigold, Billy, Coralon, and Kaleb finally arrived. "You look like you could use some help," said Marigold, breathless.

"Yes," Austin said.

Billy jumped up and flew through the air, somehow still energetic. "Die turkeys!" he yelled. He launched countless yeeter bombs.

Pretty soon, they thought they had defeated all the Baranas in that area. But then countless more swooped out the fortress wall. "Reinforcements!" yelled Marigold.

Slime pounded the ground like hailstones. All the kids could do was dodge until it was possible to attack without being glued to the ground. But Austin wasn't sure if that time would come. He wasn't even sure he would survive dodging for long.

We sure could use Thomas' glowy thing.

Mikey lifted off the landing pad on top of the zoobaquel fortress, fuel tank full. He upped his speed and held the wheel steady.

The trip wasn't long. In about five minutes, Mikey had rejoined the battle, except now he was firing on the swarms of Baranas. Specifically firing on the Baranas swarming the faropas.

The Baranas didn't expect it and were cut to pieces by Mikey's lasers. Mikey looked out the window. *What the?* he thought. The faropas were smiling and...waving!

Mikey moved on and attacked the Baranas swarming a group of relros. The relros were leaping up and biting at the Baranas. Baranas fell to the ground, poisoned by the gelro Mikey was once afraid of, but was now grateful for.

Mikey fired his lasers. The Baranas were a little more prepared this time, but their fire and slime did little but put green smudges and scorch marks on Mikey's drone.

Mikey blasted the Baranas to bits and moved on to the next group of Baranas. These Baranas were closer to the fortress's edge, fighting some furtigos that, surprisingly, weren't led by Billy.

Mikey fired on the Baranas, partially peppering the wall, which was weakening, and would cave in soon.

The Baranas turned, their single eyes going wide when they saw him firing. Next thing they knew, well, they didn't think anything else. They just disintegrated in a blast of fire.

The warning light started flashing. *Another target lock?* Mikey thought. *But I thought all the Barana ships were destroyed!*

Mikey heard a thump on the roof of his cockpit. He looked up and saw...

"Thomas?"

CHAPTER TWENTY-NINE

Thomas' face was smooshed against the cockpit glass of Mikey's drone. Thomas saw all the controls on the dashboard, and he found it pretty cool to see what was behind all the drone awesomeness. But he needed to get back to battling King Barana.

Mikey was looking up at him, confused. "I need you to drop me on the roof of the fortress!" Thomas yelled.

Mikey looked up at him, still confused. He yelled again, louder. Mikey nodded this time, and Thomas was soon back up on the roof of the fortress.

"I thought you were dead!" growled King Barana, surprised.

"Lucky for me," Thomas said. "I have a friend who learned how to fly a drone in about 30 seconds."

"Well, that friend of yours better be getting ready for the enslaving of the multiverse!" King Barana roared. His serpent-tentacle hissed and shot lots of lightning at Thomas.

Thomas smashed his body into King Barana before he could be electrocuted. Then he began to glow.

"Huh?!" King Barana said.

Thomas smiled as the glowing spread. King Barana looked boggled.

King Barana's wings disappeared. "AUGH!" he shrieked. "WHAT HAVE YOU DONE TO ME?!"

"I've glowed," Thomas replied, smirking.

It seemed the slime storm would never stop. Marigold felt like she had played 6,000 soccer games without taking a drink of water. But she had to keep moving. The slime storm wasn't stopping, so she wasn't stopping.

The slime storm grew stronger. "We need to retreat!" Marigold said. She knew they couldn't, though. They'd be glued to the spot. But the slime storm began to let up until it was just the effect of a drizzle. She turned, confused.

"Hey!" one of the Baranas said. "I ran out of slime!"

"Me too!" another agreed. "I should've eaten more slime essence for breakfast!"

"I knew doing this slime storm was a bad idea!"

"But it was *your* idea!"

"No way, man! It was *yours*!"

"Since when?"

"Since you came up with it!"

"Oh, come on, guys! Why didn't you eat enough slime essence? We knew the battle was coming!"

"Well, *you* didn't either!"

"That's because my brother ate it all this morning!"

"Well, where is he?"

"How am I supposed to know?"

"You say you know everything, that's how!"

"It's your fault!"

"No, it's *your* fault!"

Marigold began to crack up. She burst into a laughing fit, and soon Austin, Billy, and Jane had joined in.

"See, now they're embarrassing us!" the first Barana said.

"Yeah, because *you* came up with the stupidest plan in the history books!"

"It's not even in the history books!"

"Who cares?"

"I do!"

"So what?"

"So now I am going to eat you!"

The Barana swooped towards the other. "I'm gonna get you!" he yelled.

Other Baranas joined in. Soon all Marigold could hear was, "Tag! You're it! Tag! You're it!"

Marigold was starting to get annoyed by all the bickering, even though it was funny. "Can you make them stop?" she asked Jane.

Jane nodded. In no time, all the Baranas were sucked up into a portal, stuck in some void dimension, probably still bickering.

But more were on the way.

Mikey was on a roll. He'd defeated a lot of Baranas without having his drone affected. Now he was battling another group of them.

These Baranas had a different strategy than the others he had battled, though, and it was much more efficient.

They were attacking his engines with slime. Mikey managed to dodge almost all of them, but now his engines were beginning to fail. One more slime attack and he would have to crash land.

Mikey tried to escape, but there were too many. Pretty quickly, they hit again. He hadn't noticed the quiet hum the drone had been making until it stopped, and he began to fall.

He slammed all the buttons, struggling to stay aloft. He was dropping fast. He gave up and tried the repulsors. They failed too. He was going to have to crash land.

Mikey lifted on the wheel. He leveled out a little bit, but it did nothing to control his uncontrollable dive.

He held firm to the wheel. He watched as the ground zoomed up to greet him... *CRASH!*

King Barana roared with rage, unable to fly. He bounced around on his serpent tentacle, which let out short hisses of pain every time it hit the roof. Each time it coiled up and then launched upward, sending King Barana flying.

"You puny kid!" he roared. "You can never defeat me without the jewel!"

"I may be puny," Thomas said. "But I can still destroy you!"

"Not without the jewel!" King Barana growled. "I will destroy you before you ever get it!"

Then Thomas got it. He didn't have the jewel. All his attacks were worthless, and there was no way he could get it. King Barana was immortal.

King Barana began a full-scale attack. He launched a huge fireball.

Thomas just stood there. "Aren't you going to run?" King Barana growled.

"Of course not!" Thomas said.

"Then you will die!"

The fireball slammed into Thomas. He struggled not to fall over, but it didn't hurt him. "I'm fire element," he explained, smirking.

"Wha?" King Barana was confused. "You're just a puny kid! Nobody can survive a King Barana fireball!"

"Well, except for me," Thomas said.

King Barana was enraged. "NOW YOU WILL BE DESTROYED!"

"Or maybe you will be."

Mikey struggled to climb out of the cockpit. He didn't know how he'd survived, but he'd managed to come out of the crash landing with only a few scrapes and bruises.

His drone was not doing so well, though. It had been reduced to flaming hunks of metal. *I so wanted to take that home,* Mikey thought.

But he had no time. Before he knew it, the Baranas were swarming him. *I think it's about time I use some powers,* he thought.

Mikey brought up a colossal tsunami, carrying almost all the Baranas with it. *Take that!* he thought.

The rest of the Baranas fell to his laser sword. He found himself looking around for his friends. Then he spotted a portal just before it closed. *That must be where Jane is!* he thought.

He jogged over to where the portal was. He found Jane, Marigold, Billy, Austin, and that wolf Coralon there, along with a bunch of other kids.

"Hi!" he panted.

"Mikey!" said Jane. "We thought you were dead!"

"Well, here I am," Mikey said.

"But your drone crashed!" Marigold said. "How did you escape all the burning metal?"

"I don't know," Mikey replied. "When I woke up, I somehow ended up in the perfect position!"

Another wave of Baranas poured out of the fortress. "Well, here we go again," Austin said.

Thomas looked around, searching for the origin of the voice. He turned around and saw... "Sonya Speaker?" She was a few years older than when she was when she left, and Thomas had only seen her occasionally when she was in sixth grade and he was in third grade, but it was definitely her. Her wavy blonde hair was matted and tangled from being a prisoner of the Baranas for three years, and her clothes looked tight on her and were damaged badly.

"That'd be me," Sonya replied.

"Why are you here?" King Barana growled.

"To give Thomas this!" Sonya explained, digging through a backpack.

She pulled out... the Jewel of Order!

"Careful!" Thomas said. "Only the most powerful people in the multiverse can hold that!"

"No worries," Sonya said. "I have Jewel Gloves. So I can't use it, but it can't disintegrate me."

"I think I will be taking that," King Barana growled.

"Uh, no," Sonya said, tossing the Jewel to Thomas.

It was heavy, and Thomas could feel it vibrating. But it all felt too easy. Why wasn't King Barana coming to take it?

As if on cue, he burst forward, his serpent tentacle reaching out. Thomas didn't have enough time to react. He tried to spin, but the serpent's head bonked into the Jewel.

The Jewel fell out of Thomas' grip. He reached for it, but it clinked to the ground. And before Thomas could do anything, King Barana grabbed it.

CHAPTER THIRTY

Marigold had an idea. "Guys," she said. "I think it's about time I turn into a dragon."

Marigold thought of her turning into a dragon. She felt tingly, like when her foot was asleep, but this time all over her body. Her vision blurred, but she felt no sensation of transforming. She thought it wouldn't work until her stomach did a somersault, and she was a dragon.

"Whoa! This is cool!" Marigold tried to say, but all that came out were soft growls. *I must not be able to talk when in animal form,* she thought. She was a huge dragon, with shimmering green and brown scales.

She flapped her wings and flew towards the Baranas. "Hey! It's a dragon!" one exclaimed.

Marigold took a deep breath and then exhaled. She expected to breathe fire, but instead, rocks flew out of her mouth. *That must be the result of being earth elemented,* she thought.

The rocks slammed into the swarming Baranas, crushing them. The Baranas that weren't hit attempted to flee. But Marigold took another deep breath, and before she knew it, those Baranas were crushed, too.

Ten minutes later, after destroying many of the Baranas, she landed, and was human once more. She smiled at her friends. "You're welcome!"

<hr />

Thomas struggled, punching King Barana over and over. "Give me the Jewel!" he yelled in frustration.

Finally, Thomas got a good angle. He kicked King Barana's massive eye. He howled in pain, dropping the Jewel.

Thomas snatched it up, panting. "You think you've won!" King Barana cackled.

King Barana held up a remote control. Actually, the snake attached to the bottom of him held the controller in its mouth. It was a small gray box, with an antenna and one large red button. "Time to control your friends," said King Barana.

"What the heck is that?" asked Thomas.

"It's the Transformal 3000!" cackled King Barana. "It will turn all you wimpy kids into lava monsters to take over the multiverse!"

"Why now?" said Sonya. "I thought you wanted all the kids in cages for the occasion."

"That was my original plan, but I was getting impatient," King Barana explained. "Anyway, the multiverse shall be taken over!"

Thomas leaped at King Barana, trying to steal the remote from his serpent tentacle. But he shot lightning at Thomas, and he was thrown back, weak.

"Let's get this party started!" hollered King Barana. He pressed the red button.

A sound erupted from the controller that sounded a little like feedback from a microphone, but much louder. Thomas clapped his hands over his ears. He knew this sound would turn him into a lava monster...but why wasn't it affecting him?

Thomas turned his gaze to Sonya, who was crouched down, hands over her ears, wincing. She felt the wave, or whatever it was, and she was trying to fight against it. Thomas could only imagine how horrible it felt.

After she stopped fighting, Sonya had somehow not transformed into a lava monster.. "What the heck?" said King Barana. "How did you not transform?"

"No idea!" said Sonya.

Then Thomas heard a boom. He looked behind him.

Thomas was high up on the ruined roof of the Barana fortress, but he could see the lava monsters perfectly.

Austin screamed and started to run. The kids he and his friends had been helping had just turned into massive lava monsters, and they were advancing!

"Why are they lava monsters now?" exclaimed Jane. "I thought King Barana wanted all of them in cages!"

"I guess he got impatient!" yelled Austin.

The lava monsters were coming closer and closer. Austin tried to use his lightning to attack them but to no avail. They were just too powerful.

But then he got an idea. Water! "Mikey!" he said. "Hit them with water!"

Mikey nodded and launched a full-scale tsunami at the monsters. They shrieked and stomped out of the water, but it did no damage. "Uh oh," Austin said.

But Mikey did something anyway. He surrounded Austin and everyone else in water. The lava monsters tried to come close, but the water held them back.

Mikey was having trouble. "I can't hold it much longer!" he said.

Then it all went downhill. The water suddenly evaporated from the heat of the lava monsters. The kids were vulnerable. The lava monsters advanced.

Thomas saw the water protecting his friends vanish. Half the monsters attacked his friends, and the other half began to scale the walls.

The first one reached the top, lava dripping from its massive fangs. It swiped at Thomas, and he narrowly avoided it. Lava dripped from its hand and formed a pool of lava.

Thomas glowed, and the pool of lava vanished. But the lava monsters were still advancing on him and Sonya. King Barana watched it all with a smirk.

Almost 20 more lava monsters climbed over the edge. They charged at Thomas.

Thomas dodged out of the way of most of the attacks. But then something he really didn't expect happened. Beams of lava fired from the lava monsters' hands!

He tried to dodge, but they were coming too fast. In seconds, he and Sonya would be covered in lava! Even with fire powers, there was no way he could survive that!

Thomas managed to dodge the first wave of lava, but an even stronger one would come in a few seconds. He didn't know how he would defeat these lava monsters. Even with seven less lava monsters than King Barana had planned, those were the creatures that were supposed to help the Baranas take over the multiverse. How was one kid going to defeat them all?

Thomas continued dodging the lava and glowing to make pools of lava vanish. He tried using his powers and weapons a few times against the lava monsters, but to no avail.

Then Thomas remembered. Back in the clashroom when he still didn't know other universes existed. When he screamed so loud the clashroom shook. He only had one more chance. And he took it.

"LEAVE ME ALONE!" he screamed. It was even louder than when he had screamed back in the clashroom.

The lava monsters reared back and scrambled back down the wall of the fortress. Thomas peered over the edge and saw all the monsters on the ground, slowly transforming back into kids.

"How did you know that was the antidote?" King Barana roared.

Thomas didn't bother to answer. He just turned around and pointed the Jewel at him.

Thomas didn't know what he did, but a bright, blue-green beam ejected from the jewel, slowly disintegrating it.

The beam hit King Barana, pushing him back on the collapsing roof, towards the hole that would dump him into the lava of the throne room.

But eventually, the entire Jewel disintegrated. King Barana cackled. "Even the Jewel cannot destroy me!" he growled.

Thomas smiled. "Oh, but it didn't need it to. I just needed it to weaken you for me."

King Barana was confused for a second. But then he realized what was happening. With all his lighting and fire attacks, he had created the slightest dip in the roof. And all the lava flowed down into it.

That gave King Barana no chance. All around him, the roof sizzled, and then disintegrated.

That included what he was laying on, momentarily paralyzed by the jewel's attack. He plunged towards the lava.

The last words King Barana said before he hit the lava were, "Uh oh..."

PART FIVE

Back Home

CHAPTER THIRTY-ONE

When King Barana hit the lava, there was a gigantic explosion. Lava sprayed up.

Thomas launched himself off the roof just before the roof under him collapsed in. But he never hit the ground. "Huh?" he said.

Then he realized Marigold was levitating him *and* Sonya! They slowly came down to the ground.

"Did you defeat King Barana?" Jeff asked, running over from controlling the cannon.

Thomas didn't answer. He still couldn't absorb the fact that he had defeated King Barana all on his own. It was bamboozling.

Finally, after a long pause that seemed like forever, Thomas spoke, "Yeah. I guess I did."

"YOU DID IT!" screamed Dana, rushing at Thomas. She enveloped him in a big hug.

"You don't seem very excited," Mikey accused.

"But, where's Geon?" Marigold asked.

Thomas' eyes filled with tears. "He... he didn't make it," he stammered.

"Oh no!" Marigold said. "I'm so sorry, Thomas."

Billy walked over and gave Thomas a big hug. "But you did it, Thomas!" he said, actually calmly. "Geon saved you."

"He's right," Austin added. "We should honor Geon."

"So, Thomas, can you tell us the story?" Marigold asked.

"I'm just...tired," Thomas yawned. "I'll tell you the story after I get some sleep, not to mention some yorga goo."

Then Thomas realized that Samantha and Horsey were there! "Where did you guys come from?" Thomas asked.

"We heard the news of the battle. We came to see if you guys had won!" Horsey said.

"Let's go and celebrate!" said Samantha.

"Woot woot!" shrieked Billy, who was not the tiniest bit tired.

"After we get some rest," sighed Thomas.

"Of course," said Jeff.

They all headed off to the zoobaquel city. Before they left, Thomas stared up at the remnants of the Barana fortress. It was so menacing.

After they all got some sleep, they partied. It was a fantastic party, with dancing and tacos and plenty of yorga goo. In short, it was the best party of Thomas' life.

As they all sat around eating yorga goo, Thomas told them the story of how he defeated King Barana.

After they had all finished gaping at Thomas' story, Austin told the story of the battle Thomas had missed. Then Billy retold it in his much crazier yet still exciting version.

After a bit more partying, Thomas asked. "How do we get home to our universe?"

"Turns out," Samantha said, "After you guys told me about it, I decided to go looking for it. I wasn't on Mt. Tambox specifically, but in a village nearby. The people didn't care if I took it, so I did!"

"Awesome!" said Austin.

"So, it does exist," said Thomas.

"Now we don't have to go all the way to Mount Tambox!" said Mikey.

"I *don't* want to go in that gross cave again," said Jane.

"Don't worry, you won't," giggled Marigold.

They all walked outside, and the Universe Transporter was there. It looked like a giant colorful elevator, just like in Thomas' dream.

"Your universe is...SMB8437," Samantha said. "But it was renamed to Universe of Saviors."

"What does savior mean?" asked Dana.

"A savior is someone who saved something or someone," replied Jeff. "You guys did both."

"Cool!" said Dana.

Jeff pressed some buttons on the side of the Universe Transporter, and it opened. "Get in!" he said.

"Let's all say bye first," said Thomas.

"Good idea!" said Jeff.

They said bye to Samantha first. "Bye," Thomas said. "Thanks for helping us."

"Bye," said Samantha. "Have a good time in your home universe! I hope I'll be able to see you again!"

Goodbyes continued for a long time. But then it was time to go. So, they all climbed in the universe transporter.

Somehow all of the 47 remaining kids fit in the transporter, not to mention Burger Bob. As the door slowly closed, Thomas, Austin, Billy, Mikey, Marigold, and Jane waved to everyone standing outside the transporter. Their new friends waved back.

Then Thomas was falling through darkness like at the beginning of it all. But Thomas was no longer scared. In fact, he had never noticed until now how peaceful and quiet it was. When he saw the light below his feet, he smiled. *Time to return home, after saving the multiverse.*

Then they were all back in the clashroom. But now that the Baranas were defeated, it had been restored to an ordinary classroom. The classroom was empty. Everyone went outside.

Apparently, only a few hours had passed since Thomas had left because it looked like it was the end of the day. Parents were picking their kids up, and some kids were heading to after-school programs.

Of course, everyone saw Burger Bob. Almost everyone screamed and ran away. Some people just stood there, mortified.

"Don't be scared!" Billy yelled. "Burger Bob will not eat you! He is a good furry tigo!"

Despite what Billy said, the looks on people's faces didn't change much. They still looked terrified.

Thomas and Dana eventually found their mom, who hadn't seen Burger Bob. "Hi, kids!" she said. Thomas and Dana got in the car.

"So how was your day at school?" said Mom as she pulled out of the parking lot.

"Ordinary," Thomas said. "Just ordinary."

ABOUT THE AUTHORS

GAVIN BENT lives in New Mexico with his parents, sister, and dog, Aspen. He is in middle school and loves skiing, hiking, and hanging out with friends. He loves astronomy and plans to save any proceeds from this book to buy a telescope. He had so much fun co-authoring *The Clashroom* and is planning on writing more books in the future.

MAIRA FINN is in middle school and has autism spectrum disorder. She has always loved writing stories, and this is her first book published but not the first one she has written. She lives in New Mexico with her parents, brother, sister, and dog.

105 Publishing LLC
www.105publishing.com
Austin, Texas

Made in the USA
Middletown, DE
20 September 2021

48648987R00156